J. E. Casely Hayford's

Ethiopia Unbound

J. E. Casely Hayford's

Ethiopia Unbound

A Critical Edition

Edited by Jeanne-Marie Jackson
and Adwoa A. Opoku-Agyemang

Michigan State University Press | *East Lansing*

Michigan State University Press
East Lansing, Michigan 48823-5245

Library of Congress Cataloging-in-Publication Data
Names: Hayford, J. E. Casely (Joseph Ephraim Casely), 1866-1930, author. | Jackson, Jeanne-Marie, editor. | Opoku-Agyemang, Adwoa A., editor. | Hayford, J. E. Casely (Joseph Ephraim Casely), 1866-1930. Ethiopia unbound.
Title: J. E. Casely Hayford's Ethiopia unbound : a critical edition / J.E. Casely Hayford ; edited by Jeanne-Marie Jackson and Adwoa A. Opoku-Agyemang.Other titles: Ethiopia unbound
Description: East Lansing : Michigan State University Press, 2024. | Includes bibliographical references.
Identifiers: LCCN 2024002633 | ISBN 9781611864960 (paperback) | ISBN 9781609177652 | ISBN 9781628955262
Subjects: LCSH: Hayford, J. E. Casely (Joseph Ephraim Casely), 1866-1930. Ethiopia unbound. | Ghanaian fiction (English)—20th century. | Africa—Fiction. | LCGFT: Fiction. | Novels.
Classification: LCC PR9379.9.H38 E84353 2024 | DDC 823.912—dc23/eng/20240117
LC record available at https://lccn.loc.gov/2024002633

Book and cover design by Anastasia Wraight
Cover art: Colored African Fabric, Diversity Studio, Adobe Stock

---

Visit Michigan State University Press at www.msupress.org

Contents

Foreword

Gus Casely-Hayford

Joseph Ephraim Casely Hayford was one of a remarkable generation of West African intellectuals. They witnessed and then responded to a passage of profound and devastating change. And they responded by crafting some of the most important African literature ever published. They had seen firsthand the destabilization and the dismantling of the continent's indigenous states by European powers, witnessed the theft and industrial-scale exploitation of their lands by colonial administrations, and suffered the indignity of the forensic control of their peoples and then eventually the deconstruction of the spiritual fabric of the cultures they loved. Yet when the Great War called, Africa responded. It would be upon West African soil that the first shots of the war would be fired, along East African shorelines that the earliest significant naval battle would be fought—the continent's young would volunteer to fight, and be commandeered to act as porters, medics, and guides. Casely Hayford and his peers initiated the fundraisers to acquire the earliest Allied reconnaissance planes that would fly over German lines. Hundreds of thousands of Africans would be drafted and dragooned, and upon their literal backs the war would eventually be won. Although some two million African workers, soldiers, and porters would lose their lives on battlegrounds in Africa and abroad, Britain and her allies would offer little ultimate acknowledgment or reward for the continent's profound sacrifice.

Although British betrayal was heartbreaking, it did not surprise. This generation of West Africans understood the asymmetry of the colonial deal;

they had smelled the corrupt underbelly of the grand empire narrative more than a generation beforehand. They had in the earliest manifestations of the colonial plan grasped the intensity of its racism and the poisonous hierarchies that underwrote its economic agenda. But they had the sophistication to understand that while Europe's African territories were won by Gatling gun and canon, their autonomy and dignity would best be regained in law courts and through an unrelenting campaign waged upon the bigger stage of international political opinion. It would be through words of legislation and petitions that Africans would seek to build their own beachhead in response to Empire. A generation of West African scholars, journalists, and lawyers would create an undeniable momentum for change. But to meaningfully oppose a consortium of the most powerful empires the world had ever seen, Africa needed allies; they needed to feel the ambient political wind at their back. The continent's intellectuals understood that the first campaigns of this war would be won by beautifully crafted and compelling narrative. It would be narrative that spoke to the plight of voiceless peoples of color, that contextualized their frustration with hope drawn from the precolonial past and the postcolonial global future. This would be narrative with the power to speak beyond history, to transcend time, yet be a clarion call, an articulation of the anguish of a particular moment.

Casely Hayford had sensed the growing global momentum for change. In his 1903 book *Gold Coast Native Institutions: With Thoughts upon a Healthy Imperial Policy for the Gold Coast and Ashanti*, he posited how Britain might recalibrate its control of West Africa to allow space for indigenous dignity and subsidiarity. Though catalyzed by hope, written into its premise was a pragmatic accommodation of imperial control. But by the middle of the decade there had been an ambient shift in global politics, the ignition of an ember of possibility for change, as across the globe, once-tiny flickers of opposition began to combine into an unanswerable global concatenation.

Within a very brief passage of months, Freud began his *Three Essays on the Theory of Sexuality*, Einstein published his first paper on relativity, and Henry Ford became convinced of the possibility of a mass-market car. The opening years of the twentieth century began to shape a new cultural narrative and set out the terms of a new political age. In that tiny calendar window of the century's first decade, Picasso would create *Les Demoiselles d'Avignon* and imagine abstraction beyond, and Stravinsky would begin exploratory work catalyzed by jazz. These dazzling intellectual and creative innovations seemed to stand in contrast to so much of what had gone before—and yet felt simultaneously timely.

If the Enlightenment moment had seemed to be founded upon a very particular set of hierarchies and inequalities, driven by the will and the well-being of a tiny blessed few, then this moment was an Old Testament climacteric. It was like Isaac, defying destiny to unbind his son, to emancipate the incarcerated innocent, a forcing of a fundamental ontological adjustment of our understanding of authority and the importance of previously marginal voices. This was not just a freeing up of systems and beliefs, but also the beginning of a wider discussion about individual rights, played out through the changing expectations of women, workers, peoples of color, and the colonized subjects of Empire.

These were seismic shifts in modes of understanding and ways of living that rewrote the geometry of global politics. The Western project required a new post-Enlightenment moral cosmology, a recalibration of the power balance of geography, gender, and race. It was a moment that gave birth to new writing, anthems, new heroes, new points of inspiration. Picasso and Freud would look to Africa for their muses, Stravinsky to jazz, each searching simultaneously for the reassuringly old and the radically new, each seeking to resolve dialectical tensions in creative ways.

And it seemed only right that once-stifled African voices would find their own place in building a new intellectual compass with which they might rechart the world. As *Les Demoiselles d'Avignon* was a paradigm shift, a move from trying to resolve the physics of the visual, to trying to come to terms with its metaphysics, so Casely Hayford in his great pan-African opus *Ethiopia Unbound* would seek like an archaeologist to reimagine a continent's past and reset its relationship to the future. It was a novel, but it was also a philosophical toolkit, a mechanism by which we might not just excavate and reanimate lost history, but craft the tenets for a different kind of future. In the face of the pervasive ambient vision of a backward-inward-looking Africa, this was radical, revolutionary, uplifting—but it was also beautiful. Not a fist-thumping revolutionary *tractatus*, but an elegantly confident and sophisticated literary instantiation of long-overdue self-realization.

J. E. Casely Hayford became a bridge between the generation of his father, whose political consciousness was formed amid the scramble for Africa, and the generation of his son Archie, whose friends and political allies would wrest freedoms and independence back from Europe. He found ways to capture the pain and frustration, yet to craft a metaphysical manifesto that spoke of hope and possibility. In the face of so much acculturated damage, beautiful words would offer a welcome lifeline. He understood, like Fanon, that "mastery of language affords remarkable power," and *Ethiopia Unbound* would describe more than dream of an emancipated Africa; he did not just implore Africans to fight for their freedom but crafted an apparatus to imagine how they might deliver it. Rooted in African metaphysics and epistemologies, he linked the continent's precolonial past to a glorious, emancipated future; he conceived an African narrative, catalyzed by indigenous knowledge, not defined and shaped by others. And from the continent's intellectual archaeology, he conjured a spiritual compass to orientate and guide its populations to rebuild systems of confidence and hope.

As we reread Casely Hayford's words today, *Ethiopia Unbound* feels both of its time and a work reborn. In our age of populism and political polarization, its implicit establishment of timeless principles by which to live, in its inherent celebration of equity, of cultural pride and respect for those that went before, in showing responsibility to those that will follow, *Ethiopia Unbound* feels deeply, refreshingly relevant. In the tone with which it is conceived, its measured humility, its aspiration for a ceaseless search for greater understanding, *Ethiopia Unbound* offers us worthy values by which to shape futures. Its core aspirations are of tomorrow: they are of hope, of belief in the promise of the African continent, of the deliverance of a moment when the world's power and resources are more justly recalibrated. Though the realities of many Africans' lives continue to be tainted by the pervasive legacies of colonialism, the twenty-first century undoubtedly belongs to the continent. The future belongs to its young growing populations, to its burgeoning economies, to its irrepressible energy and creativity. Today the pervasive culture of global youth is in many ways a diasporic culture—the world's beats, its rhythms, its environmental ethics and sustainability ethos are African. The arms of pan-Africanism have stretched out beyond the continent to embrace and touch us all, to become so ubiquitous, so exquisitely ambient that many of us simply accept them as our future. Though there is so much to do, and so many frustrations remain, with so many profound challenges ahead, the dream of *Ethiopia Unbound* is upon the wind. In many ways that would have delighted Joseph, we are free—we are unbound.

Introduction

The historic town of Cape Coast, capital of present-day Ghana's Central Region, is breezy and serene, cramped and crumbling. It is also "busy" in ways that transcend the human traffic navigating its narrow streets—it has been built through the layering of disparate, even jarringly mismatched things. The Wesley Methodist Cathedral, one of the town's older and more august edifices, is only a few hundred meters away from the emblematic site of Cape Coast Castle, which also boasts a chapel of its own. Underneath *that* church, where colonial officers would worship on Sundays, are the claustrophobic dungeon cells where the enslaved were amassed before being shipped to the Americas between the sixteenth and nineteenth centuries. Less tragically, Cape Coast was described by J. E. Casely Hayford (1866 to 1930) as "the leading town in the Gold Coast" in one of his many publications about the region's past.* The town is a former seat of government and the cradle of Ghana's literary and political modernity, especially by way of its once-vibrant press.

At the helm of the unique Cape Coast intellectual tradition was an aspirational nineteenth-century class that brokered between European traders and colonialists on the coast and native peoples inland, and that came, for better or worse, to adopt many English cultural norms. The town thus juggles its reputation as a place of somewhat fussy and pretentious people—Western-aspiring, even—with the fact that it has less sophisticated infrastructure

* J. E. Casely Hayford, *Gold Coast Native Institutions: With Thoughts upon a Healthy Imperial Policy for the Gold Coast and Ashanti* (London: Sweet and Maxwell Limited, 1903), 260.

and resources than the present-day Ghanaian capital of Accra, or even the port city of Takoradi farther down the Gulf of Guinea coast. Its legacy as the Gold Coast's print intellectual epicenter is also its literary calling card. *The Blinkards*, a 1916 satirical drama by the Cape Coast writer Kobina Sekyi, puts its double-edged identity as a small-time metropolis, of sorts, into bold relief. The play called for a revival of the local language and culture among the burgeoning Western-educated class, while satirizing their excessive colonial affectation.*

Wesley Methodist Cathedral, with its high walls and clock tower, sits atop Cape Coast's Chapel Square and overlooks both the Atlantic Ocean and Cape Coast town. Methodism entered the Gold Coast via Cape Coast in 1835, and this building was erected by locals and missionaries together "laboring on, spending and being spent," to paraphrase a Methodist hymn from that period. An extract from the "One Hundredth Report of the Methodist Missionary Society, Gold Coast District," published in 1935, highlights "clearly the elements which continually recur in the history of Methodism on the Gold Coast: a daring plan of campaign, a fellowship of service in the Way wherein missionary and African helper each make their contribution, a dark cloud of fatality." Indeed, many of the Europeans dropped like well-intentioned but ill-equipped flies within a few months of arrival on the Gold Coast, due mainly to unfortunate run-ins with malaria. Perhaps because the church plays up that history, entering it can be a slightly disorienting experience. One moves from an open, sunlit courtyard into a cozier but also much darker, restrictive interior. Narrow paths then expand to a grand pipe organ and altar, under which are buried the remains of early British proselytizers.

* The play was part of a movement called "Gone Fantee," which emphasized the importance of local customs and traditions. An article from the *Gold Coast Methodist Times*, dated September 30, 1897, and titled "Reasons for the Resumption of Native Names," illustrates the pervasiveness of this concern. Fante, housed within the larger Akan meta-ethnicity, even has the perfect word to affix to the people who inspired Sekyi's colorful cast of characters: "*aborɔfosem*," from the root words "*aborɔfo*" (foreigners from overseas) and "asem" (in this case, mannerisms).

Neither Cape Coast nor Wesley Methodist Cathedral is a metaphor, exactly, for the novel *Ethiopia Unbound*. It is nonetheless edifying to have a sense of some of the things that the town and church reflect about Casely Hayford's generation of Fante intellectual leaders, and that they, in turn, share with the text: pokiness; an eclectic hodgepodge of elements; an alternating emphasis on obscure spirituality and rational modernization; and an underlying ambition to ascend, transcend, and guide. Furthermore, to enter Wesley is to inhabit a timeline of key events in Cape Coast history, owing not least to the familiar Fante surnames on the plaques adorning its walls—Ward Brew, Ekem Ferguson, Awotwi Pratt, Annobil, Hayfron, De Graft Johnson. Casely Hayford would say that Cape Coast had "within its walls the best intelligence of the country" (*Native Institutions*, 260). Indeed, some of the memorial descriptions in Wesley Cathedral evoke period-specific terms and institutions, like the "educated African," the Aborigines' Rights Protection Society, the National Congress of British West Africa, and the Gold Coast Legislative Council. The founders and members of these groups, intellectuals born during or soon after the lifetime of a fledgling mid-nineteenth-century, African-led state called the Fante Confederation (1868–1874), sought to create organizational infrastructure to advance their cultural and political leadership. Compared with those at the forefront of later anticolonial struggles (most famously, Ghana's first president, Kwame Nkrumah), they have sometimes been viewed ungenerously as too demure and too prolix. To look deeper, however, is to see ambitious leaders who were both ahead of and constrained by their time. They complicate the meanings we may now ascribe too broadly to certain African historical keywords: intelligentsia, élite, nationalist.

The Wesleyans played an important political role in the conjoined Africanization of Gold Coast Christianity and politics. Casely Hayford's grandfather, father, and brother—James Hayford, Joseph de Graft Hayford, and Mark Christian Hayford—were all Methodist ministers. Casely Hayford himself attended Cape Coast's Wesleyan High School and later headed the Accra Wesleyan boys' high school. Partly owing to the Methodist emphasis on formal education, the members of the Cape Coast intelligentsia carved into history on the Wesleyan Cathedral's walls often aggravated British colonial administrators, who expected a more docile local population. In the opening pages of his 1913 treatise *The Truth About the West African Land Question*, Casely Hayford bemoans the "frequent cry," in the colonial Gold Coast press, of "the educated African." He calls it "a childish cry—a sign of weakness" that stems from resistance to "the assertion of individuality, on the part of the African."* As Casely Hayford saw it, when the British sneered at Fante leaders' Western credentials, this was a way of using a standard of African "authenticity" to disguise their fear of African equality.

Ethiopia Unbound does not conform to a conventional understanding of the novel form, which emphasizes narrative development and character cohesion, but rather choreographs and combines different rhetorical modes. It moves swiftly across philosophical and political debates, fictional episodes, and cultural and religious lessons, all loosely tied together by a learned protagonist meandering through its pages. That figure, named Kwamankra, spends much of the text mulling over spiritual affairs. At the same time, he is focused on the nuts and bolts of their workings in his consciousness. *Ethiopia Unbound* paints the "city of the ancient dead," for instance, as a place that transcends earthly preoccupations, yet the text pays scrupulous attention to the layout of the city and its underlying logistical mechanisms: How does one enter? How is it organized? The Gold Coast leaders of the people of "Ethiopia"—which meant all members of the black race—are, here, equally concerned with their spiritual ascent and with building a sturdy ladder to enable the climb. At the same time, the narrative dedicates important space to detailing Fante concepts and traditions, such as in Kwamankra's explanation of the word *Nyiakropon*—Fante for God—to an English friend. To Casely Hayford's generation, to be a member of the Gold Coast élite was to be concerned with the management and orchestration of even the most intangible things.

* J. E. Casely Hayford, *The Truth About the West African Land Question* (London: C.M. Philips, 1913), 3.

Ethiopia Unbound was published in 1911, and is by most accounts the first novel published in English by an African writer.* Unsurprisingly, it is deeply concerned with what it means to be "African" (or "Ethiopian") at the dawn of the twentieth century, on the cusp of no less than epochal historical change. In retrospect, Joseph Ephraim Casely Hayford—also known as Ekra-Agyeman—is often viewed as a "proto-nationalist" figure: one who saw the presence of Gold Coast Africans within colonial political institutions as a stepping stone to independence from British rule. But while this neat version of events suggests a pleasing continuity between nineteenth-century cultural self-invention and the anticolonial triumphs that followed, it also obscures the confusions and tensions that *Ethiopia Unbound* expressed in its own moment. The early years of the new century were marked by intense debate about the rightful locus of African—and world—authority. It is easy to counterpose tradition with modernity as concerns, for instance, the codification of lived Fante cultural practices in written form. It is harder to track the shifting alliances between people and groups that laid claim to both tradition and progress in a period when their virtues were closely intertwined. Casely Hayford was one of the most prominent of such people, and was involved with all of the most influential such groups.

Practicing law in West Africa, in his lifetime, was not only a specialized career; it was also the mark of a new and capacious regional social profile that gathered literature, legislation, education, and spirituality into a single nation-building agenda. While Casely Hayford was one of the Gold Coast's first barristers, he was already part of a fledgling intellectual and political tradition. George Eminsang, the first European-educated lawyer to work in the Gold Coast, negotiated the infamous transfer of Elmina Castle from Dutch to British control in 1872. This preceded British declaration of the Gold Coast as a colony (rather than a protectorate) in 1874, upsetting so-called

* As Stephanie Newell has pointed out in *Literary Culture in Colonial Ghana* (2002), this label overlooks some serialized romances and connected tales published in Gold Coast newspapers prior to this date, usually anonymously authored. A single page from an 1888 issue of *The Gold Coast Echo*, to take one example, contains a chapter from *Marita: Or the Folly of Love. A Novel. By a Native* and *Fanti Tales: Anansa's (the Spider's) Pretended Death.*

educated Africans' notions of intra-imperial partnership and fueling their ambitions to self-determination. Self-documentation was a crucial part of this goal, and legal training offered a vocabulary with which to weave a far-reaching and sophisticated narrative of Akan democracy.

Casely Hayford's closest peer in this task was John Mensah Sarbah, who was born, like him, in the small town of Anomabu outside Cape Coast and whose major publications—*Fanti Customary Laws* (1897) and *The Fanti National Constitution* (1906)—coincided with Casely Hayford's own. Their shared choice of written form was what one might call the legal-humanistic treatise. Casely Hayford's 1903 *Gold Coast Native Institutions: With Thoughts upon a Healthy Imperial Policy for the Gold Coast and Ashanti* intersperses detailed descriptions of Akan customs across domains including marriage, succession, and property distribution with commentary on Gold Coast history and cultural character. Far from being merely a dry recitation of customary precedents, it argues outright for their present political salience. At various moments in the text, Casely Hayford berates the British government for "an insane thirst for territorial acquisition," as well as its "harmful" and "useless" efforts to "set back the onward tide in the progress of a nation under its protection." British legal expertise was thus bound up with an assertive new brand of African print opposition. Casely Hayford and Mensah Sarbah were teachers as well as lawyers, staid institution builders as well as firebrands.

The lists of Casely Hayford's and Mensah Sarbah's affiliations are nearly identical, and likewise span priorities on legislative process and liberal education. Mensah Sarbah, too, attended Cape Coast's Wesleyan High School, and was later the driving force behind its absorption into and renaming as Mfantsipim. The two men worked in tandem to build an agile African-led institutional network, wielding their pens and highbrow credentials to redress British colonial overreach and pompous misunderstanding. In 1897, Casely Hayford and Mensah Sarbah were among the cofounders of the Aborigines' Rights Protection Society (ARPS), and in 1902, of the Fante National Education Fund, an initiative dedicated to cultivating a prestigious but locally attuned set of Gold Coast secondary schools and colleges. From this, eventually, would grow not just Mfantsipim but the equally revered Achimota College (originally known as the Prince of Wales College and School). Founded in 1927 as the Gold Coast's first coeducational boarding school and with Casely Hayford on its board of governors, Achimota especially championed so-called vernacular learning. Its annual general report from May 1928 lists classes offered in Twi, Fante, Ga, and Ewe, as well as the number of staff members who successfully qualified in each language by way of exams administered jointly by Achimota itself and the Gold Coast Education Department. Fante comes out on top, with six staff certifications listed.

For its part, the ARPS was inarguably the most significant Gold Coast political organization of its time. Its most urgent and successful fight was against the Lands Bill of 1897, whereby the British claimed jurisdiction over what they wrongly thought to be empty territory; ARPS pressure resulted in the Concessions Ordinance of 1900 and a reversion to the rule of customary law. Yet ARPS activities also increasingly bore the mark of the Gold Coast's internal tensions, particularly when the British implemented a policy of indirect rule in 1912. As colonial leadership sought favor with local chiefs to do its bidding, the organization's work was arrested by divisions between their leadership and that of the new, Western-educated legal class. In its ushering of mission-based into professionalized models of African print modernity, the achievements of the Fante intelligentsia in the mid to late nineteenth century resonate with those of the early New African movement in South Africa.*

* The New African Movement is often thought to begin with Tiyo Soga (1829–1871), a journalist, minister, and intellectual who is best known now for his translations of the Bible and John Bunyan's *Pilgrim's Progress* into his native isiXhosa. Soga was educated at the Lovedale Missionary Institute in present-day South Africa's Eastern Cape, an institute that was founded in 1841 and became an educational hub of a similar order to Mfantsipim in Cape Coast or Fourah Bay in Freetown. Also like the Fante Confederation's afterlives, the New African Movement extended through the middle of the twentieth century, ending around 1960 and culminating in the multifaceted intellectual career of Es'kia Mphahlele (1919–2008). Ntongela Masilela's authoritative study of the movement, *An Outline of the New African Movement in South Africa* (Trenton: Africa World Press, 2013), is included in the "Suggested Further Reading" list in this volume.

Nonetheless, the ARPS's crisis of purpose was already evident in 1911, as made clear by an unsigned article in the May 27th edition of the *Gold Coast Leader* titled "The Raison d'Etre of the Gold Coast Aborigines Rights Protection Society." Ironically, Casely Hayford and his ilk defended their loyalty to the British crown in order to rebut accusations of self-serving elitism. The article begins verbosely: "The scandalizing credulity which operates in certain quarters that the Gold Coast Aborigines Rights Protection Society is an indigenous organization engineered by a few irreconcilable and irresponsible revolutionists whose one absorbing mission in life is to offer, at all times and under all circumstances, strenuous and persistent opposition to His Majesty's Government, right or wrong makes it imperatively necessary that the declared objects of its existence should once more be published, if only to disabuse the minds of those who may be led away by such disparaging legend and unfounded dogma." The ARPS cause *is* the true Gold Coast cause, it wants to say, as testament to which fact its leaders endorse the choice of their "Ancestors hundreds of years ago [to voluntarily] associate themselves with the British Government."

It is perhaps no wonder that *Ethiopia Unbound* weaves such a tangled web of interests and affinities: Casely Hayford's national credibility demands an imperial vow, with his ability to serve as "the mouthpiece of the people" certified by His Majesty's Government. In the broadest terms, his and many of his peers' politics could be categorized as simultaneously anticolonial and pro-imperial, a tense pairing of sentiments that also animates the novel. In a chapter called "Signs of Empire: Loyal Hearts," Casely Hayford writes, "The Gold Coast is also a component part of the British Empire—as necessary to the complete whole as the smallest link to the complete chain." While such emphasis on the shared mission of colonized and colonizer may strike today's reader as odd, Fante leaders in particular had long viewed themselves as partners with, rather than beholden to, the British in the Gold Coast, in government as well as in faith. This was most notoriously expressed by an agreement called the Bond of 1844, whereby a group of Fante chiefs signed over criminal legal jurisdiction to British authorities. In the ensuing decades, and up to the moment of *Ethiopia Unbound*'s publication, Fantes bemoaned the British betrayal of this collaborative understanding of their relationship. Perhaps naively, Casely Hayford did not see Britain's increased consolidation of power in the late nineteenth and early twentieth centuries as an obvious or inevitable outcome of its history in the region.

The flourishing Gold Coast press, based largely in Cape Coast, provided the main outlet for African criticism of imperial policies. It is possible that Casely Hayford wrote that 1911 article on the ARPS in the *Gold Coast Leader*, since he cofounded the paper in 1902. His journalistic activities also spanned other publications. His uncle edited one of the first newspapers in the Gold Coast, the *Western Echo*, which Casely Hayford later took over and renamed as the *Gold Coast Echo*. These papers, along with the *Gold Coast Methodist Times* and the *Gold Coast Nation*—the official papers, respectively, of the local Methodist church and the ARPS—became hotbeds of African-led political protest and commentary. Editorials on official matters both local and imperial were interspersed with speech transcripts, serialized narratives, and more idiosyncratic features. The *Nation*, in the latter category, had a "News in Brief" section with short updates on recent events, while the *Methodist Times* ran brief "Great Thoughts" capsules on subjects like "How the Chinese Do Things" (an arbitrary example from November 1897). Beyond his various editorial and author roles, Casely Hayford often appears in these accounts of Gold Coast comings-and-goings, mostly arriving from and departing for London by ship. The press, in this way, was key to consolidating his stature and intellectual milieu, positioning him as a public figure as well as a journeyman writer and policymaker.

It is unsurprising, then, if *Ethiopia Unbound* underscores and even hyperbolizes the reach of Gold Coast newspapers. Here, the press is not only in the mundane business of providing information; it also plays a moral role. For example, the final chapter foresees an intellectual revolution, central to which will be the *Gold Coast Nation* and *Ethiopian Review*. The press is to act as a catalyst for a future "wind" blowing across the world, molding the spirits of nations and awakening Ethiopians to take up positions as thoughtful world leaders. Here too, even amid great fervency and the occasional religious image, the narrative takes care to highlight the practical building blocks of this new order. The process entails the circulation of newspapers and the promotion of the interests of the Gold Coast national conservancy, then grows to "embrace the needs of the entire race." In the thick of things stand the men at the helm of the press: the newspaper editors, in tandem with *Ethiopia Unbound*'s protagonist Kwamankra. Their role is to oversee new developments while in dialogue "with the leading thinkers of the race throughout the world."

That larger-than-life quality also characterized Casely Hayford himself, a sought-after patron in different areas. Newspapers represented only one aspect of his command over the public scene; social and literary clubs represented another. These clubs and societies were created and frequented by young men along the West African coast from the nineteenth century onward, and the Gold Coast birthed more than its fair share of them. Members met to read and discuss literary texts, analyze and debate social and moral topics, and mingle with like-minded, Western-educated people at meetings, soirées, and even balls. Clubs were a means to learn and assimilate European cultural elements—such as eveningwear, debates in English, ballroom dancing, and so on—and a way of exhibiting one's mastery over these things.

Over the decades, the clubs grew to include more members from beyond the most elite ranks of Gold Coast society. These youths possessed varying levels of education but held similarly high ambitions as the sociopolitical landscape transformed around them. At any point in the clubs' history, therefore, it was advantageous for them to be associated with a man of Casely Hayford's stature, given his remarkable track record as an institution builder and man of culture. Thus, the Cape Coast Literary and Social Club, founded in 1914, did not hesitate to broadcast Casely Hayford's position as their patron. One printed program from the period, which advertises "Dances, Conversation, Musical Games, Speeches & Toasts, Theatrical Performances," puts this profile-raising function in bold relief. The card accords as much space to listing the upcoming events as to naming the club's twelve patrons, and places Casely Hayford directly after His Excellency the Governor and the Provincial Commissioner. In a different document dated April 11, 1921, the Cape Coast Literary and Social Club requests the use of the Government Gardens from the Commissioner of the Central Province: the club would like to organize a reception to celebrate the safe return from England of "the Honourable Casely Hayford, M.B.E., Barrister-at-Law and [Patron] of our Club."* On November 22, 1930, the same club would hold a memorial service at the Varick Memorial Hall to commemorate their late benefactor, following his death in August of the same year.

We might, as implied so far, attribute Casely Hayford's convictions and achievements to his privileged background. After all, he was of ruler stock. His family belonged to the prestigious Fante *anona* (parrot) clan or *ebusuakuw*, one of seven such inherited affiliations, and was well positioned in Cape Coast hierarchies and Gold Coast politics. His father, Joseph de Graft Hayford, was an outspoken religious and political player. A founder of the Fante Confederation, he was even arrested by British administrators on charges of conspiracy when he continued to champion the confederation's cause after its formal dissolution. His grandfather, one of the early converts to Methodism and the bearer of an important royal title, played political roles for traditional rulers and even died in the exercise of one such duty. Casely Hayford's mother, Mary Brew, was the descendant of an Irish merchant profoundly invested in the Gold Coast—both commercially and in a more personal sense, by marrying a Fante woman. His older cousin, James Hutton Brew, wrote the first draft of the Fante Confederation constitution.

* That particular wish was met with a refusal: a response from the Provincial Commissioner's office lets it be known that the day and time requested "synchronise with the hour at which the Europeans have their tennis recreation."

If Casely Hayford's path to success was not set at his birth in 1866, then it was certainly inaugurated by the formidable education that followed. He was one of the Wesleyan High School's first and most famous alumni. The school was later rechristened as the renowned Mfantsipim and is perhaps best known today as the former United Nations Secretary General Kofi Annan's alma mater. Mfantsipim's origins link Methodist education directly with a zeal for intellectual argument as an anticolonial tool. In "A Record of the Beginnings and Development of Mfantsipim, Issued as a Memento of the 75th Anniversary of the Founding of the School," written in the early 1950s, its then-headmaster, F. L. Bartels, makes special note of the fact that "the debate as a medium of instruction [in the 1890s] particularly in History received much emphasis." Casely Hayford then graduated from Fourah Bay College, Sierra Leone, which was founded in 1827 as the first European-style university in West Africa (it was affiliated with England's Durham University until the 1960s).* After working for a while as a teacher and secondary school principal in the Gold Coast, he left to read law and economics at Peterhouse, Cambridge. He was called to the bar at London's Inner Temple in 1896, and soon after returned to Cape Coast. He established a successful law firm there and then in Axim and Sekondi, further along the Gold Coast's western seaboard.

But Casely Hayford's background alone cannot account for the triumphant bizarreness of *Ethiopia Unbound*. It is a text whose most basic identity

* Fourah Bay is at the heart of a rich tradition of West African leadership extending beyond Casely Hayford's lifetime, which allows for a broader appreciation of his regional significance. The Reverend Thomas Babington Macaulay, for example, an affiliate of the college, in 1859 founded the CMS Grammar School, the first (and now oldest) secondary school in Lagos. One of CMS's many illustrious graduates was Nnamdi Azikiwe, who served as the first president of independent Nigeria between 1963 and 1966. Azikiwe is in many ways a successor figure to Casely Hayford. In addition to his statesmanship, immersion in Gold Coast politics in the 1930s, and interest in African philosophical and cultural regeneration, he founded numerous prominent nationalist newspapers, including the *West African Pilot* in 1937.

is constantly called into question, a "novel" whose adherence to even a minimal definition of that form is ever in doubt. As Molefi Kete Asante writes in his introduction to the 2011 edition of *Ethiopia Unbound* published by Black Classic Press, "One could approach the book as a novel, a philosophical treatise, a dialogue of rationalism, an Edwardian Romance or as a meditation on love of self, family and community. It is all of these and more because it is filled with Greek myths as reference and is a sound political tract on the contemporary strivings of the Turks and Russians as well as British colonial life."* In its journeying across treatises, speeches, romantic episodes, parables, and paternal conversations, *Ethiopia Unbound* also rebuffs any clear ideological consistency: it freely draws on biblical language while eschewing Christian practices, and promotes black capability and independence while at points professing reverence for the British Empire.

Some of this variation, to be sure, can be attributed to Casely Hayford's scattershot compositional methods, which entailed republication of his own journalistic work within the novel's imaginary confines. Some of its fictionalized episodes also seem to end as abruptly as they began, with characters who seem important simply dropping out of the narrative or suddenly reappearing, long after their debut. (Chapter 2, for instance, opens on a young woman named Ekuba and closes when she storms from the scene. Almost out of the blue, she is revisited eleven chapters later, then never appears again.) What unites the pages of *Ethiopia Unbound* is thus its disposition or manner. This might best be described as a propensity for moral, intellectual, and spiritual dignity that borders on grandiose, but that is wed always to the hard-nosed organizational emphasis discussed earlier.

The first pages of the novel announce the sheer scale of its ambitions for Africans' rebuttal of the degrading image painted of them by Europeans. Casely Hayford writes of the "black man" that "Here was a being anatomically

* J. E. Casely Hayford, *Ethiopia Unbound* (Baltimore: Black Classic Press edition, 2010), introduction.

perfect, adaptive and adaptable to any and every sphere of the struggle for life. Sociologically, he had succeeded in recording upon the pages of contemporary history a conception of family life unknown to Western ideas. Moreover, he was the scion of a spiritual sphere peculiar unto himself." A tremendous amount hinges on this line, which compresses many sources of identity, as well as conceptions of sovereignty, into the slim phrase "unto himself." From it a host of tricky questions arise. How, exactly, do the autobiographical particulars of Casely Hayford's life—the clear template for *Ethiopia Unbound*'s main character—inflect and combine with more far-flung intellectual influences? Where is there friction between, and where smooth synthesis of, Western and African, or black and European, spiritual and political traditions? To what degree can the novel's projections of an imagined future, especially in its final chapter set in 1925, be read not just as a liberation fantasy but as a rekindling of real nineteenth-century Fante state-building achievements?

Ethiopia Unbound does not offer ready answers to any of these lines of inquiry. What it does do is to lay out a wealth of material from which to craft different responses to them. In Casely Hayford's hands, Africanness is at once situated and protean. He is acutely attuned to his particular Fante lineage, returning to it always as a linguistic and cultural touchstone—this includes providing a glossary of Fante key terms at the start of the text. At the same time, he eagerly entwines Fantes' pride of place in his imagination with the full range of his intellectual interests. Two paragraphs after his ebullient description of the "perfect" and "adaptive" black subject, he lists, as "sons of God among them," the names of prominent late-nineteenth and early twentieth-century black artists and intellectuals from across the Atlantic world: W. E. B. Du Bois, Booker T. Washington, Edward Wilmot Blyden, Paul Laurence Dunbar, and Samuel Coleridge-Taylor. Collectively, these figures are meant to conjure a "distinguished . . . intellectuality" that testifies to what should now be black men's privileged role in British imperial glory. They are poets and scholars, composers and institution builders, all proof of a greatness carved against the grain of white underestimation.

Some of these interlocutors' relevance to Casely Hayford's leadership agenda is especially direct. Du Bois founded America's National Association for the Advancement of Colored People (NAACP) in 1909, and, like Casely Hayford, enjoyed great prominence as a writer and editor, most famously of that organization's official magazine, *The Crisis*. He was also a powerful advocate for a politics that connected continental Africans with the African diaspora, especially through his involvement with what has become a legendary series of Pan-African Congresses beginning in London in 1900. (Thirty-three years after Casely Hayford was buried in Accra, Du Bois too would die in the capital of what had then become an independent Ghana.) Booker T. Washington, born into slavery in Virginia in 1856, was the foremost American exemplar of Casely Hayford's educational goals. For thirty years, he led Alabama's innovative Tuskegee Institute in developing a robust university curriculum for black students and fostering a self-sufficient campus life. Washington's success with Tuskegee helped to inspire Casely Hayford's vision for Mfantsipim, which he hoped would grow from a secondary school into a national university on the order of Fourah Bay College in nearby Freetown, Sierra Leone. The most significant of the names listed as "sons of God," however, is no doubt Edward Blyden. After emigrating to Liberia from the Danish West Indies (now the U.S. Virgin Islands) in 1850, Blyden accrued a loyal intellectual following as a writer, scholar, and diplomat. Casely Hayford was exposed to Blyden's philosophy of the "African personality" and unique civilizational development during his own time at Fourah Bay, and *Ethiopia Unbound* bears its heavy imprint.

The novel's boldest invocation of Blyden's profile is also used to pinpoint the evolution of Casely Hayford's own racial worldview through Kwamankra's comparison of black American and pan-African intellectuals. Chapter 16 of *Ethiopia Unbound*, "Race Emancipation—General Considerations: Edward Wilmot Blyden," begins by praising the white American educationist Samuel Chapman Armstrong for his work leading the Hampton Institute, a foundational black (and later, Native American) college in Virginia where Kwamankra is said to be giving a speech on Blyden's work. But while Casely Hayford as the chapter's unnamed narrator is enthusiastic about Hampton's intellectual life, Kwamankra's speech criticizes America's limitations. "The work of men like Booker T. Washington and W. E. Burghart Du Bois is exclusive and provincial," he pronounces. "The work of Edward Wilmot Blyden is universal, covering the entire race and the entire race problem." African American ambitions, the speech then maintains, are too concerned with remapping the lines of white American achievement. Through Blyden's work, "the black man is engaged upon a sublimer task, namely, the discovery of his true place in creation upon natural and national lines."

To some degree, Blyden's influence can also be seen in Casely Hayford's shifting institutional goals and loyalties. In the decade after *Ethiopia Unbound* was published, he sought a political venue with transnational aspirations but that also maintained real, on-the-ground regional traction—somewhere between, that is, the multicontinental vision of the Pan-Africanist Congresses and the Gold Coast-specific activities of the ARPS. A far-reaching thinker and writer, Casely Hayford was nonetheless ever alert to the risks posed by distance and abstraction to good governance. In a speech to the Gold Coast Legislative Council in 1919, he affirms the importance, in determining bureaucratic compensation, of such decisions being "left in the hands of local bodies who [know] all the circumstances and conditions of the place." Furthermore, as power struggles between Fante chiefs and Casely Hayford's legal-technocratic class grew more pronounced with the advent of British indirect rule, the time was ripe for him to branch out in other directions. Through the latter half of the 1910s but solidified with its first conference in 1920, Casely Hayford and a number of peers thus founded a new organization called the National Congress of British West Africa (NCBWA). Casely Hayford served as its first vice president, with Thomas Hutton-Mills as president. It was Casely Hayford's stature, however, that was widely viewed as the NCBWA's linchpin. In a 1920 report to England's King George the Fifth, the Gold Coast governor's deputy C. H. Harper notes that "The Conference owes its inception and realisation mainly I believe to the efforts of Mr. Casely Hayford."

The NCBWA's earliest documented aims were particular to its moment, and included winning British resolve against returning any of Germany's former African colonies to its control, as well as the total abolition of "liquor traffic" in West Africa due to fears about alcohol abuse. Its lasting achievement, however, was to have constituted, from Africa, a multinational body with a functional bureaucratic structure determined to guide British imperial policies. At the same time, a younger generation of Gold Coast nationalists—including *The Blinkards*'s author Kobina Sekyi, also a member of the NCBWA—was growing impatient with Casely Hayford's incremental approach to change. Even at this point, Casely Hayford's objectives for racial development and self-determination were wed to a commitment to intra-imperial collaboration; he was not a racial separatist, and saw nationhood as constituting just one part of a reasonable whole. In a different speech to the Legislative Council in 1919, titled "The Treaty of Peace," Casely Hayford remarks that the loyalty of the Gold Coast people to the King "is not merely a matter of sentiment or lip-service, but loyalty built upon an intelligent basis." Harper echoes this impression in his 1920 report, noting that "It was not possible to detect in the augural [NCBWA] address or in the speeches in support of that address any sense of acute grievance" against the crown.

If the strands of Casely Hayford's thought outlined thus far do not seem to add up to a consistent and summarizable set of views, it is nonetheless their eclecticism and even dissonance that form the lifeblood of *Ethiopia Unbound*. This is doubly true of the vast range of influences and references brought into the text drawn from far afield of what is often called the Black radical tradition, or any explicitly racial line of thought. Nor are these other influences limited only to Western classics, even as what Stephanie Newell sums up as "discussions of Shakespeare, Dickens, Bacon, Ruskin or Eliot" would have been *de rigueur* for Casely Hayford and other Gold Coast literary club members of his era.* Casely Hayford's range of erudition is truly global, and

* Stephanie Newell, "Paracolonial' Networks: Some Speculations on Local Readerships in Colonial West Africa," *Interventions: International Journal of Postcolonial Studies* 3.3 (2001): 336–354, 346.

deeply dynastic in its display: his references rove across Japanese Shintoism (an animistic belief system), Shakespeare's *Hamlet,* Peter the Great's expansionist achievements, and Marcus Aurelius. Japan is a recurring point of fascination for what Casely Hayford sees as its ideal balance of national consciousness and worldly openness. At one point, he declares that "The Japanese, adopting and assimilating Western culture, of necessity commands the respect of Western nations, because there is something distinctly Eastern about him. He commands . . . the uses of his native tongue, and has a literature of his own, enriched by translations from standard authors of other lands." And these intellectual coordinates are just the beginning. The text is also littered with references to long-forgotten philologists and poets.

Going back farther in the history of imperial civilizations, *Ethiopia Unbound* also reroutes the supposedly Western legacy of antiquity through the novel's lens of African leadership. Its penultimate chapter is titled "A Similitude: The Greek and the Fante." In it, Kwamankra endorses the study of Greek and Latin alongside that of local African languages, and remarks on the familiarity of Ulysses's experience of hospitality and ritual in *The Odyssey* to a Fante sensibility. The cultural affinity between the Greeks and the Fantes is expressed in openly spiritual terms, as Kwamankra presents a comparison of their respective deities: the Fante *Niakrapon* and the Greek Zeus, as well as the Fante *abusum* with the Greek "lesser gods." Elsewhere in the text, Casely Hayford underscores the spiritual essence of African political enfranchisement through the model of Jewish exile and rebirth. "How extraordinary would be the spectacle of this huge Ethiopian race—some millions of men—," he enjoins, "having imbibed all that is best in Western culture in the land of their oppressors, yet remaining true to racial instincts and inspiration, customs and institutions, much as did the Israelites of old in captivity!" The cumulative effect of *Ethiopia Unbound*'s allusiveness is to portray Fante uniqueness as a worldly composition formed across centuries, a river charging forward fueled by tributaries from all ends of the earth.

The idea of gathering many sources into one force also serves here as a good point of departure for the novel itself in the pages that follow. Many commentators on Casely Hayford, as on colonial-era African intellectuals broadly, describe his politics and worldview through the lenses of contradiction or paradox. This is understandable; it is not intuitive in the postindependence era to imagine the complementarity of African self-determination and British imperial loyalty, or canonical erudition and indigenous activism. Still, emphasizing how things do not—or should not—make sense together can sometimes direct focus too far away from the mechanics by which they nonetheless do. The neat package of "contradiction" is, moreover, especially unsatisfactory in view of Casely Hayford's abiding investment in practical details and logistical feasibility. Instead, and with some distance from both Casely Hayford's political imperatives and those of newly independent Ghana in the mid twentieth century, we might retrain our attention on how *Ethiopia Unbound* precisely choreographs its far-reaching interests.

To appreciate the subtleties of J. E. Casely Hayford's Cape Coast origins, Gold Coast institutional investments, and his expansive humanistic reading in interlinked form is, at heart, to tune into the importance of the novel as a distinctive form of expression. While *Ethiopia Unbound*, with its autobiographical resonances and journalistic cuts-and-pastes, is not "pure fiction," neither is it a simple rehashing of the political and historical views Casely Hayford proclaimed elsewhere. Instead, it is a proposal for how to connect who he was with who he wanted to be: a Gold Coast exemplar of a new African mind, a Fante name reclaimed in the name of a world to come.

J. E. Casely Hayford's

Ethiopia Unbound

A Glossary

Omanhin: Head of a state or king, plural Amanhin.
Kruba: A vessel for carrying light articles; in this case for collecting money.
Nanamu: The gods of the Fantes.*
Nanamu-Krome: The abodes of the gods.
Sanko songs: Sea songs.
Wankora wonkor: Without whom not, an idiom signifying Leader of Leaders.
Effua Kobi: The Mother of Calcali, King of Ashanti, before the war of 1873.

* In Casely Hayford's text, this was originally spelled "Fantis." Where it is not part of the title of a published work, we have changed it here and throughout the volume to what is now the standard English spelling of "Fante" to avoid confusion. The name of this second-largest language group within West Africa's Akan meta-ethnicity has also frequently been spelled Mfantse (its Fante spelling) and Fantee (a colonial variant). Casely Hayford wrote during a period of intense discussion surrounding the status of Akan languages, particularly with regard to whether Fante and Twi—the language of the inland Asante people—were to be separately standardized or simplified into one language called Akan. British colonial linguists favored the latter option, while Fante intellectuals resisted the absorption of their language into a single grammar. The spellings of many Fante terms listed in the original text of *Ethiopia Unbound* were likewise inconsistent or in flux. We have standardized the spelling where there is no question of meaning. In the case of *Nyiakropon* (God), however, about whose origins and standard spelling there has been substantial debate, we have retained the variations from the original text. In his classic *The Akan Doctrine of God*, for example, published in 1944, J. B. Danquah notes that Casely Hayford's explanation of the term is "theologically rather than etymologically sound."

To the Sons of Ethiopia
the World Wide Over

Do not believe that you know a people
if you have not ascended to their gods.
*—M. Edgar Quinet**

* Edgar Quinet (1803–1875) was a prominent and versatile French intellectual best known for his work on the French Revolution and religious nationalism, as well as his first French translation of the German philosopher Johann Gottfried Herder's influential 1774 text *Reflections on the Philosophy of the History of Mankind* [*Ideen zur Philosophie der Geschichte der Menschheit*]. Though Quinet is little read today outside France, his interests in a grand scale of political progress and the relationship between culture and religion clearly converge with those of Casely Hayford.

CHAPTER I

An Ethiopian Conservative

At the dawn of the twentieth century, men of light and leading both in Europe and in America had not yet made up their minds as to what place to assign to the spiritual aspirations of the black man; and the nations were casting about for an answer to the wail which went up from the heart of the oppressed race for opportunity. And yet it was at best an impotent cry. For there has never lived a people worth writing about who have not shaped out a destiny for themselves, or carved out their own opportunity.

Before this time, however, it had been discovered that the black man was not necessarily the missing link between man and ape. It had even been granted that for intellectual endowments he had nothing to be ashamed of in an open competition with the Aryan or any other type. Here was a being anatomically perfect, adaptive and adaptable to any and every sphere of the struggle for life. Sociologically, he had succeeded in recording upon the pages of contemporary history a conception of family life unknown to Western ideas. Moreover, he was the scion of a spiritual sphere peculiar unto himself; for when Western nations would have exhausted their energy in the vain struggle for the things which satisfy not, it was felt that it would be these people to whom the world would turn for inspiration, seeing that in them only would be found those elements which make for pure altruism, the leaven of all human experience.

Again, the art of the caricaturist had by now been played out. It was no longer possible, as far as this race was concerned, to depict the Sultan of

Zanzibar, for example, other than as an Ethiopian gentleman, "clothed and in his right mind."

And there were sons of God among them, men whom the Gods visited as of yore; for even now three continents were ringing with the names of men like Du Bois, Booker T. Washington, Blyden, Dunbar, Coleridge Taylor and others—men who had distinguished themselves in the fields of activity and intellectuality—and it was by no means an uncommon thing to meet in the universities of Europe and America the sons of Ethiopia in quest of the golden tree of knowledge.*

Here, in London, about the time of which we write, were to be seen two young men, walking arm in arm up Tottenham Court Road, and, ever and anon, stopping to examine old dirty books in some second-class bookstall, or some quaint relics in a curiosity shop.

Presently, the twain stopped at a particularly ancient looking bookshop off a by-street leading to Upper Bedford Place. The darker man of the two picked up from the stall outside, a well-thumbed copy of Marcus Aurelius, and began carelessly to turn over the leaves. Suddenly he stopped, and his face grew pensive. Turning to his friend, he said, "Isn't it funny, Whitely, the remarkable similarity of thought and almost of expression there is between all the great teachers of the past? Listen to what, for instance, Marcus Aurelius says here,"

* W. E. B. Du Bois (1868–1963), Booker T. Washington (1856–1915), Edward Wilmot Blyden (1832–1912), Paul Laurence Dunbar (1872–1906), and Samuel Coleridge Taylor (1875–1912) were all well-known Black intellectuals who straddled the nineteenth and twentieth centuries, as well as interests in politics, education, and the arts. They are notable in aggregate here for the range of Black geographies they introduce to the text, which spans the United States, the West Indies, West Africa, and England. Notably absent from this list of names is the Jamaican pan-Africanist Marcus Garvey (1887–1940), founder of the Universal Negro Improvement Association and African Communities League in 1914. Though Garvey had later organizational ties to Adelaide Smith Casely Hayford in her work as an educationist in Sierra Leone, J. E. Casely Hayford had ambivalent feelings toward the politics of Black diasporic return to Africa. In the official correspondence of the National Congress of British West Africa, for example, he writes, "[Returnees] have no idea of our laws and institutions, nor as to our rights of property, and they may seek to get into touch with us by some channels that are not the right ones."

reading aloud a paragraph from the *Meditations*, which ran thus: "'Pray not to save thy child, but that thou mayest not fear to lose him.' Now, you, a Divinity student, what do you make of that?" And without waiting for an answer, he added, "Does it not read very much like the teaching of the holy Nazarene—'he that findeth his life shall lose it,' or words to that effect? Now, what I wish to know is what had Jesus Christ in common with Marcus Aurelius?"

"Candidly, Kwamankra," said Whitely, "I have never given the matter a thought; but since you put the question, and viewing it from a merely debatable standpoint, I am inclined to say that the first question to consider was whether Jesus Christ was man or God."

Kwamankra raised his eyes in astonishment. "You do surprise me, Whitely; how can you, of all others, have any doubt upon the matter? I thought you were going up for Orders."

Whitely appeared confused, but soon regaining composure, he said to his companion, "Let us move on."

As they sauntered along, Whitely began: "You know, Kwamankra, I can talk better walking, and I will now answer the question you put to me a while ago. At one time I thought of taking Orders, and even now I may do so. But a little evil in the shape of an unanswerable doubt haunts me by day and night, and it is even the self-same question I put to you at the bookshop."

"Well, I hardly know what to say, Whitely. In these matters, I, of course, regard myself as an outsider. You see we pagans come all the way here to sit at the feet of Gamaliel," he said with a little mischievous laugh, "and it is uncommonly hard upon us for you to entertain doubts upon the broad questions upon which we seek comparison and light. But I can conceive of no such difficulty as you experience in our system. Jesus Christ man or God?" he repeated slowly and musingly unto himself—then turning somewhat suddenly to his friend, he said, "You know, Whitely, since I learned your language, not as a vehicle of thought, but as a means of more intimately studying your philosophy, I have been trying to get at the root idea of the word 'God'; and so far as my researches have gone, it is an Anglo-Saxon word, the Teutonic form being *Gutha*, which is said to be quite distinct from 'good.' Whence then, one may ask, come your ideas, as associated with the fountain of all good, of omnipresence, omniscience, omnipotence? Of course they are borrowed from the Romans, who were pagans like ourselves, and who, indeed, had much to learn from the Ethiopians through the Greeks."

A turn or two took the young men to Russell Square, and soon they found themselves at Bedford Place. The darker man of the two produced a latch-key, and invited his companion to come in. There was nothing remarkable about the rooms except that they were furnished in the Oriental style. Here and there, at convenient comers, were divans with rich cushions, embroidered in silk, and carpets of leopard skins into which the feet sank as one walked. On the walls were trophies, consisting principally of African weapons. There were to be seen a collection of musical instruments of all descriptions, some so simple as to make one wonder how any symphony could be got out of them. A well-filled shelf, with a plain oak desk, littered with written matter, with some flowers here and there, about completed the outward circumstance of the room into which our visitor was ushered.

Pushing well forward the only easy chair in the room, and placing his friend in it with a smile of welcome, he threw himself upon a low seat beside him, touched a bell on a side table, and ordered some refreshment.

"I hope you don't mind my old-world ways," remarked Kwamankra. "You know, though I have lived in this country fairly long, off and on, I like to sniff a bit of the African air somehow where'er I go."

"That is perfectly natural, at least with a well-balanced mind," correcting himself, said Whitely; "but what I can't understand is that you don't seem a bit Eastern in your methods of work. To judge from that pile yonder," eyeing the notes mischievously, "one wouldn't think you were over here for a holiday."

"Oh, that is only a bit of derivative work. You have no idea how interesting it is. Would you like to see what I am doing?"

"How good of you! I should be delighted."

"I shall soon be finishing now," said Kwamankra excitedly. "You see I am at the letter 'Y.' And that reminds me: you remember a while ago my taking you to task over the feebleness of the idea of 'God' in the Anglo-Saxon language.

I have just got the corresponding word here in *Fante*. It is a big word, so big that you can hardly manage it:—

NYIAKROPON.

Does it convey any meaning to you? How can it? And yet, I can assure you, my friend, it is no mere barbarous jargon. It is the combination of distinct root ideas in one word. It relates back to the beginning of all things visible, and links the intelligent part of man with the great Intelligence of the universe. Breaking up the word into its component parts, as I have done, we have:—

Nyia nuku ara oye pon. That is,
He who alone is great.

"How very suggestive. Who should have thought it?" observed Whitely, enthusiastically.

"Well, let us take the next word, then,

NYAMI,

which is still more suggestive, and analyze it. Broken up, it stands in bold relief thus:—

Nyia oye emi. That is,
He who is I am.

Now compare the Hebrew *I am* hath sent me, and you have it. Nor is this a fanciful play upon roots, for our people sing unto this day:

'Wana si onyi Nyami se?'
Dasayi wo ho inde, okina na onyi,
Nyami firi tsitsi kaisi odumankuma.'

meaning:

> *'Who says he is equal with God?*
> *Man is to-day, to-morrow he is not,*
> *I am is from eternity to eternity.'*

"You can now understand," continued Kwamankra in a low, sad tone, "why your difficulty surprised me. But now that I come to think of it, it may be due to the limitations of your language."

"After what you have just shown me, I must confess there is a deal in what you say; and somehow you Orientals manage to keep your hold on the eternal verities, where we flounder and are lost."

"Pardon me, my good friend, not quite that. As yet you are only drifting, drifting, drifting away from the ancient moorings that you Westerners built in sand. Jesus Christ came from the East. In Bethlehem he was born, and in Egypt was he nurtured; and, yet, you seek to teach Him us. We have caught His Spirit and live; you follow the letter and are tossed hither and thither by every wind. Forgive me when I say that the future of the world is with the East. The nation that can, in the next century, show the greatest output of spiritual strength, that is the nation that shall lead the world, and as Buddha from Africa taught Asia, so may Africa again lead the way."

"I am not prepared to dispute the matter with you, Kwamankra, and there seems to be a good deal of truth in what you say; but how about the doubt deep down in my own heart? That is a personal affair, you know. In a word, what think you of the Christ?"

"What a clever dialectician you are, Whitely, to be sure? If I did not know you so well, I would hardly think you were serious. You throw back to me the question I put to you a while ago, and you lay upon me the burden of solving my own riddle."

Whitely's voice was low and sad with a suspicion of emotion in his whole manner, as he said: "Forgive me, Kwamankra, if I have seemed flippant; I was never more serious in my life. I have arrived at a crisis in my career which may mean disaster at any moment; and, what is more, until this day I have never had the courage to speak it out to any of my friends for fear they would mock at my doubts."

Kwamankra turned upon his friend a look full of penetration and sympathy; and, for the moment, Whitely felt uneasy under the searching glance of the Eastern student.* It seemed to him as if in that instant Kwamankra had probed his inner nature and found it shallow.

"According to our ideas, Whitely, one broad divinity runs through humanity, and whether we are gods, or we are men, depends upon how far we have given way to the divine influence operating upon our humanity; and, comparing one system with another, I must confess there was in the man Christ Jesus a greater share of divinity than in any teacher before or after Him, and that was in my mind when I was wondering what Marcus Aurelius had in common with Jesus Christ.

"But tell me, Whitely, supposing Jesus Christ had been born of an Ethiopian woman instead of Mary of the line of David, do you think it would have made any difference in the way he influenced mankind?"

"What a strange question," returned Whitely; "our Lord born of an Ethiopian woman?"—forgetting his doubts for the moment—"Whatever put such an idea into your head? I am sure you are the first man who has given expression to such a thought."

---

* Though Casely Hayford is not "Eastern" in a geographical sense, "Eastern," "oriental," and "Ethiopian" are all used in the text to refer to African characters. While "Ethiopian" designates all people of African ancestry, "Oriental" and "Eastern" were, at the time of *Ethiopia Unbound*'s writing, used more or less interchangeably in the European public sphere to exoticize nonwhite peoples. Among the most prominent English-language anticolonial publications of Casely Hayford's time, for example—one that, according to his son Archie, he greatly admired—was a newspaper called the *African Times and Orient Review*. Published between 1912 and 1920, it was "devoted to the interests of the coloured races of the world." For a deeper understanding of the "Orientalist" idea, see Edward W. Said's *Orientalism* (Penguin Books, 1978) and Linda Nochlin's *The Politics of Vision: Essays on Nineteenth-Century Art and Society* (Boulder: Westview Press, 1991), both included in our "Suggested Further Reading" list.

"Yes, it is strange"—and there was a vibration of the intensest pathos in Kwamankra's voice—"that an African should venture to think that the Holy One of God might have been born of his race. I can easily interpret your thoughts; but, tell me, what is there extraordinary in the idea?"

"Oh, I don't know. Habits of thought, convention, and all that sort of thing, I suppose. And yet I am hardly qualified to speak upon these things," said Whitely, softening.

He rose to go. He was due farther west to see his people. Before leaving, he laid a hand on Kwamankra's shoulder, and looking gravely into his face, he said: "It is a pity, Kwamankra, I did not meet you a little earlier in my career. But even now, it may not be too late. Good-bye! Mind you meet me at Liverpool Street Station before the hour for the night train up. Good-bye!"

CHAPTER II

Sowing the Wind

Silence prevailed in the room, except for the stitch, stitch, stitch, of a woman past the early bloom of womanhood who, at first stitching merely to pass away the time, now thrust the needle viciously into the embroidery, as if bent upon drawing some secret from the heart of the silken cords of life.

Presently she began to cry—hot burning tears which flowed from the passion of a heart which sought for rest and found none.

The curtains were down, and, save a glowing fire which a young student kept poking for no reason at all, the atmosphere of the room, as far as these two souls were concerned, was in strange keeping with the fog outside. They were man and wife, these two, at least before God.* Of his own free will he had made love to her in far away Africa, and she had responded. But that was years ago. She, then, a buxom, lively lass, he an intelligent youth of the National University. She, now in England, only a nurse-maid; he a successful student, equipped and ready to carry all the world before him. Yes, they were man and wife, these two; yet were they both ill at ease, and the young man would have willingly trusted himself to the tender mercies of the London fog.

* This may also be referencing a Christian wedding. Some men would marry in a church but marry again (or already be married) by traditional rites. Though the traditional marriage might permit polygamy, such a marriage would not be recognized by the Christian church. Similarly, a wedding could be validated by the church but remain unrecognized by the bride's or groom's extended family. Sekyi's *The Blinkards* uses the rejection of a church wedding by a Fante family as an important plot point.

Yet he could not go. It was the law of compensation. He was fairly caught in his own meshes, and fate called upon him to face the music.

To do Tandor-Kuma justice, for that was the youth's name, he had always intended to remain steadfast in his promise to Ekuba. But now the circumstances were changed, and he was doing his best to grapple with a most difficult situation. How could he, a professional man, used to all the luxuries of English life and habit, take back with him to start a career in Africa a nursemaid? And what would he do, if asked to Government house? Thoughts such as these passed through his mind and made him obdurate to the pleading of the woman at his feet,

"If you cry again, Ekuba, I shall leave you. You know it is too bad when I am doing all my best to amuse you in this horribly depressing weather."

"Oh, you needn't trouble about that, Tandor-Kuma. I know you will leave me in any event. You don't think I have lived all these years without knowing what you men are. You press weak women into your service, and when you have won their sympathy, for a dream you toss them away like this," viciously kicking at the rug before the fire.

"Now, Ekuba, try and be reasonable. You mustn't think I am going to desert you. Bad as we men are, we have our ideals, and we never rest until we realize them."

"Good! That beats all the cant I have ever heard! What is the next, pray? And women have no ideals, of course! Uncultured women do not feel, do not think! They are just like clay in the hands of you men to mold—to make or mar."

"Now you are getting angry. Let us discuss this matter dispassionately."

Instead of that, Ekuba burst into a paroxysm of grief which Tandor-Kuma found it hard to control. By degrees, she grew calmer, and, sticking a pin or two in her head-gear, she snatched up her wraps and stood ready to depart.

"Tandor-Kuma," she said, "you have your ideals, and I have mine. Let us part like friends. I shall not give you the opportunity of dismissing me like a cur. Good-bye, for the present! It may be we shall meet again." And before the young student could frame a suitable answer, Ekuba was gone.

CHAPTER III

Love and Life

1.

The Mfantsipim National University had, about the time that these studies open, been already doing good work in Fante-land. It had its origin in the national movement which swept over the country in the stormy days of 1897, when the people, as if moved by a sudden impulse, rallied round the Aborigines Society and successfully established the principle of land tenure under which the country has since thriven.*

It had been felt for a long time by men of light and leading in Fante-land that the salvation of the people depended upon education; that to educate the youths of the country properly depended upon trained teachers; and that it was the work of a university to provide such training ground.

* As described in the introduction, Casely Hayford envisioned the Mfantsipim School in Cape Coast as the prototype for a new form of African schooling through the university level that would combine a Western-style liberal education, in its attention to foundational texts as well as Classical languages, with learning in local African or "vernacular" languages. Mfantsipim archival documents divide its foundational curriculum into "English" and "Extra Studies," with the latter encompassing Classics (Latin and Greek); Mathematics (Geometry and Mensuration; Algebra; and Trigonometry); Sciences (Chemistry; Animal Physiology; and Natural Philosophy); and Modern Languages (French). The "stormy days of 1897" here refers to Cape Coasters' organized resistance to the Crown Lands Bill of 1897, whereby British colonial administrators in the Gold Coast sought to take control of what they wrongly viewed as "wasted" land.

The people did not wait for endowments from the rich and the philanthropic, or for moneymaking syndicates to start the work; but quickly collecting a few enthusiastic young men, these went about from province to province and from village to village trying to instill into the commonalty what the country lost by the neglect of education. The people began to understand and to talk about the matter in the wayside places. So that when Jubilee Day came round, and from province to province throughout all the states of Fante-land the gong-gong of the *Amanhin** went round for contribution by the people to the National Educational Fund, great was the enthusiasm of high and low, and there was not a hamlet throughout the land which did not send its fair share of contribution. Even the children threw into the *Kruba*† in the market places their threepenny bits.

Among the enthusiastic band who canvassed the educational question was Kwamankra, and none more ardently than he. He was a man of remarkable intelligence, who, receiving the best education the schools of those days could afford, had, by hard work and natural taste for book-learning, so impressed the community with his ability that at the age of nineteen he had been entrusted with the editorship of the national newspaper, and had already come to be regarded as one of the coming leaders of the people.‡

Upon the opening of the National University, Kwamankra gave up newspaper work and joined the University staff. He was foremost in bringing forward schemes to prevent the work of the University becoming a mere foreign imitation. He kept constantly before the Committee from the first the fact that no people could despise its own language, customs, and institutions and hope

* The Amanhen (singular ɔmanhen) are the kings of the traditional states. Messengers ("gong-gong beaters") deliver notices to the public.

† A platter.

‡ Kwamankra here is a thinly veiled stand-in for Casely Hayford, who in 1885 assumed assistant editorship of the *Western Echo* newspaper, then owned by his maternal uncle James Hutton Brew. He was appointed as editor in 1888, at which time he renamed the paper the *Gold Coast Echo*.

to avoid national death. For that reason the distinctive garb of students, male and female, was national with an adaptability suggestive of the advanced state of society. It was recognized that the best part of the teaching must be done in the people's own language, and soon several textbooks of known authority had, with the kind permission of authors and publishers, been translated into Fante, thereby making the progress of the student rapid and sound.*

The scheme involved, as it has been shown, the turning out of efficient teachers, and as the University was affiliated to that of London and in working correspondence with some of the best teaching institutions in Japan, England, Germany, and America, the work done was thorough. A young man or woman obtaining a certificate as a trained teacher was sure of work in any part of the country at a recognized salary. Upon arriving in a province, all that the teacher would have to do would be to present his credentials to the Secretary for Education of the *Omanhin*, who, having a list of districts ready for a teacher, would at once introduce the newcomer. Generally he would find a suitable schoolhouse with all necessary appliances, but not the children; and he would be given to understand by the Committee that whether the schoolhouse remained empty or filled depended upon his own energy and the interest he brought into his work, and, what was more, his rise to the maximum stipend would be the result of the maximum success expected. As a rule, the teachers were men who had their heart in their work, and the filling of the schools was a matter of two or three months.

The thirst for knowledge spread so rapidly that men and women took to attending night schools where they quickly picked up reading and writing in their own language, and such was the general eagerness for learning that translation work had become a distinct feature of the work of the University.

---

* The emphasis on fashion in this description, alongside Fante's elevation to a language of formal educational instruction, reflects the major tenets of a trend toward cultural revitalization broadly referred to in the late nineteenth century as the "Gone Fantee" movement. In 1910 Casely Hayford helped to establish an organization called the Mfantsipim Mbofraba Feku, or Fante Youth Movement, devoted to studying and preserving the best of Fante customs and traditions, including native dress.

Hence at the time that we made the acquaintance of Kwamankra, he was engaged upon derivative work in London. His health having given way somewhat as the result of excessively hard work, he had been recommended to go away for a bit, and taking advantage of the opportunity, he had visited Japan, Germany, and America to study their methods, winding up, as he planned out in his own mind, with a visit to England.

By this time the outlook of Kwamankra upon life was broadening; and the young man was beginning to cast in his mind the most useful avenue by which his life's work could be best accomplished. While he thought upon these things, that Divinity which shapes our ends, whether we understand or no, was shaping matters in a way for Kwamankra that he could hardly anticipate. By a resolution of the University authorities, while in London, an offer came to him to continue his stay for a period of three years certain, for the purpose of superintending the publications of several standard works in the vernacular that the University had arranged to bring out. When the offer came, he at once closed with it, seeing therein a way to the fixing of his future career. And so the die was cast. Having private means of his own, he joined the University of Cambridge, read jurisprudence for a year, and having then joined the Inner Temple, had, at the time that we met him along Tottenham Court Road in the company of Whitely, settled down in London to read law in grim earnest.

2.

In the far-away home in Africa, where Kwamankra was born and bred, he had known a little orphan girl who attracted attention wherever she went by her simple, unaffected ways. She must have been under the ministration of some guardian angel, for if ever a person grew in favor with the gods and men, it was she. Daily she was to be seen in the temples of *Nanamu*,* and

* Literally "among the ancestors"; where the ancestors/gods are.

no one was more attentive, or worried the old priest afterward with such knotty questions. She was born well, and, having passed through a course in the University, was now visiting Europe for the first time to put the finishing touches to her education.

When Whitely parted with Kwamankra, the latter made his way to Holborn and wandered aimlessly down Oxford Street, his mind full of varied thoughts. He had always been a thinker, and this morning in his conversation with Whitely fresh avenues of thought had opened up in his mind which he wished to pursue undisturbed. As he watched the mighty procession of men, women, and children jostling one another, he was overwhelmed with a sense of the weariness which European civilization had evolved for itself. But it was of the teaching of the Christian philosophy and its paradoxes that his mind was full. Was it not the Nazarene who said: "Come unto me all ye that are weary and heavy laden, and I will give you rest"? Had he given this people, who professed to be his followers, rest in their constant attempt to overreach one another, in the way they trampled upon one another unto fame and fortune? Again, he had called all his followers brethren, and was not his the injunction to go forth and teach all nations that all might be brethren? And, even now, the words of Silas Whitely, Divinity scholar of Queen's: "What a strange question! Our Lord born of an Ethiopian woman!"—again rang in his ears. What if bishops, prelates, in the direct line of Him, Who made Himself of no reputation, felt the same, and yet dared to propagate his gospel among the Ethiopian Gentiles? Were there to be paradoxes all the way through? A religion which taught one thing, and practiced another, was it worth following? And in his inmost heart he found himself thanking the gods that he was a poor benighted pagan according to the formula of the Church.

In the frame of mind in which Kwamankra was, he was in no temper to be disturbed; but as luck would have it, he had not gone far when he saw coming toward him a dark man, known among his fellows as the Professor. He professed all things, and knew nothing in particular. He was in reality Kwow

Ayensu, a student of several years' standing at the Charing Cross Hospital, to whom, as far as one could judge, the question of a medical or a surgical diploma was of a secondary consideration. Kwamankra dodged the Professor, and made for the opposite pavement. The Professor as promptly crossed over, and familiarly tapping him on the shoulder, said in a gruff voice, "Hallo! old fellow, how are you? I have not seen you for quite an age; and what is the meaning of cutting an old chum like this, eh?"

Evidently there was no getting away from the Professor, and so Kwamankra resigned himself to his fate.

"The fact is," said Kwamankra, "if you want me to be frank with you, I wanted to be alone. I was so enjoying myself before you interrupted me. I love to observe without being observed."

"Do you include in your observations that of humanity in general?" dryly put in the Professor.

"Yes," replied Kwamankra. "To me it is the most interesting study, and the best theater I find to be these very pavements, the performers being the moving throng of men and women. To study humanity in this guise is to me the acme of intellectual pastime, and much as I would like a chat with you another time, I am really sorry you disturbed me."

"Your case," said the Professor, "is a simple one of cerebral contraction of the sympathies. Come with me, old boy, to the Argyle Rooms tonight, and I warrant you the finest study of humanity anywhere in London. You may notice without being noticed, and if you should feel inclined to thaw, by Jove! you will have your work cut out. Some of the latest arrivals are rare bits, and they are the rage of all the young hounds, misnamed men. Do come with me."

"I thank you for the kind invitation, but I am afraid I cannot come to the Argyle Rooms with you tonight, as I must catch the night train to Cambridge with a friend."

"Well, then, come with me to the York Hotel instead. It may be I shall be able to interest you, and, if you please, you may stand me a treat after. I hear some of you 'varsity chaps are very good that way. Your average rusty London student does not understand champagne suppers and that kind of thing."*

"If it comes to that, Professor, we needn't go all the way to the York Hotel. We can just drop in at Slater's round the corner, and I will warrant you as good a lunch as you ever tasted. Come along now. I will take no refusal."

It did not take much to persuade the Professor, and together they were soon seated at a well-appointed table in a comfortable corner. After lunch the Professor said to Kwamankra, "One good turn deserves another. I thought I would give you a bit of a surprise, but since the mountain would not come to Mahomet, I suppose he must go to it. The fact is, Mansa is in London, and is staying at the York Hotel with her father."

3.

When Kwamankra called at the hotel the next day to pay his respects he was surprised to learn that, an hour or so previously, Mansa and her father had taken the train for Harwich on their way to the Continent. The girl had always expressed a desire to see the principal countries of Europe, and as her father had a little business in the south of Germany, she had coaxed him, on the plea that it yet wanted a fortnight before she would be due to enter college, to take her with him. So pleased she was with her German surroundings, that when her father was returning to London, she was loth to come with him; and as

* It is important to note that the alliance here between Kwamankra and this more senior Fante scholar is based not only on their shared race or culture of origin, but on their class-based claim to mannered sophistication. Casely Hayford, his peers, and his immediate successors wrote frequently of the plight of educated Africans in particular—often generalized as the figure of "the educated native"—who felt under-credited within both traditional Akan and British political hierarchies. At numerous points throughout the text, Kwamankra appears to see himself as not only equal but superior to British counterparts. Casely Hayford's 1903 treatise *Gold Coast Native Institutions: With Thoughts upon a Healthy Imperial Policy for the Gold Coast and Ashanti* (London: Frank Cass, 1970), listed under "Suggested Further Reading" in this volume, provides further evidence for this disposition.

she had always shown a decided inclination for music, it had been decided she should remain at school there for a year or two to pursue her studies.*

Time passed and Kwamankra had no news of Mansa. All the Professor could tell him was that her father had returned to Africa, and the young lady was pursuing her studies on the Continent.

In the meanwhile, Kwamankra was quietly reading in the Temple. They were eventful years—those three short years in the heart of the metropolis. The science of jurisprudence had always attracted him. It opened to him vistas of justice and fair play between man and man, which strongly appealed to him. The influence of the stoical writings over the Roman jurists, producing a Law of Nations, showed him a way by which the nations of the earth, yielding to higher impulses, might mete out justice to the weak races of mankind. Moreover, the opportunity which it gave him of comparing the institutions and customs of his own country with other systems was an endless source of delight to him. Now was his opportunity to fit himself for the battle of life. He read, not for examinations, but for information. He drank freely from the vital springs of knowledge and found his soul satisfied. He could not help feeling that he had a call to duty, and that in the service of his race.

At the time of Kwamankra being called to the Bar he had invited to London for a day his friend Whitely. After the ceremony they repaired to the Haymarket to hear Mr. Beerbohm Tree in the part of Hamlet. As the curtain did not rise till 8:30, and the evening was particularly fine, they walked down

---

* This description is based on the biography of Casely Hayford's second wife, Adelaide Smith, whom he married in 1903, two years after the death of his first wife Beatrice Pinnock. Smith was a highly educated and financially self-sufficient Sierra Leonean woman of mixed English, Fante, and Creole heritage. She studied music at the Stuttgart Conservatory before meeting Casely Hayford, and in 1923 founded the Girls' Vocational School in Freetown. Smith was also a published writer, and Gladys, her daughter and only child with Casely Hayford, became a well-regarded poet. Further information can be found in Adelaide Cromwell's *An African Victorian Feminist: The Life and Times of Adelaide Smith Casely Hayford, 1848–1960* (London: Frank Cass, 1986), also included in "Suggested Further Reading" in this volume.

to the theatre from the Temple, and the conversation naturally turned upon Shakespeare's masterpiece.

"You know, Kwamankra, I have never forgotten the conversation you and I had three winters ago along Tottenham Court Road, and I have been going deeply into the matter. I have been comparing the worship of Osiris by the Egyptians of your own race, the Akkadian philosophy, the religions of Zoroaster, of Buddha, and of Confucius, the teachings of the Greek mysteries, and of the stoic writings, and the farther I have gone into the matter the more puzzled I have become as to the right of the people calling themselves Christians to a monopoly of divine light. And as to the term 'heathen,' I think it arrogant for any devotee of any one sect to apply it to another. There is as much sense in it as the ancient Greeks dubbing all others barbarians. Here we are tonight, for instance, going to hear a play written by one William Shakespeare, a Christian gentleman, who flourished in the reign of Queen Elizabeth. I dare say if I stood in the pit of the Haymarket tonight, and made an open statement that William Shakespeare was a gentleman, but I had my doubts as to whether he was a Christian, I would be hooted down and hissed out of the theatre. Yet a superficial reading of some of his works will convince you that his sentiments, if he wrote from his inmost self, which he must have done, great poet as he was, were far from those of a Christian. See how Hamlet nurses in his bosom a feeling of revenge so poignant as to find satisfaction in killing the wicked king only at a moment when he will fall with all his sins upon his head. It reads like the work of a heathen, and yet I dare not suggest that William Shakespeare was a heathen at heart."

Kwamankra burst into a hearty laugh.

"Unless you have read Jevon to little purpose, you must admit that that argument is faulty. Yet I cannot help agreeing with you that the word 'heathen' is a relative term, and perhaps your average Englishman has no right to call the average Ethiopian heathen. Ours was the cradle of civilization, and that it had not the permanence that the Christian civilization is likely to have does not make it any the less a civilization; and I, for one, feel nothing but pity for the kind of ignorance which scoffs at what it does not understand."

The speaker stopped somewhat abruptly, and eyed the listener curiously. After a second, he continued:

"You know perfectly well, my good friend, that I am not a Christian. If not, what am I? Perhaps delicacy may forbid you saying what you think. But, believe me, I am not ashamed to be called pagan, or heathen, or by any other such pet word. With all due respect to St. Paul, we worship that we do know. The fact of the case is, that from the days of the great teachers of Christianity you Christians have not taken the trouble to understand any other system but your own."

"You know, Kwamankra, turning off the subject, I have taken my degree, and I am soon due for ordination," said Whitely. "But all these years the reason and the faith within me have been in such deadly conflict as to leave my senses reeling. Yet the die is cast; I have given my name in to the Bishop; I cannot look back for fear of breaking my mother's heart."

"I am sorry for you, my dear friend," said Kwamankra, "but, perhaps, you don't look at the matter from the broad point of view that an outsider can look at it. I know, of course, something of the religions of the past. I have studied our own Eastern systems and compared them with the system you Westerns have adopted, and find that one broad divinity as well as humanity runs through them all. You will grant, I think, that there was something that lifted man to God in all the systems you have named, and in others of which, as yet, you know nothing, and that some of the founders of these systems, such as Epictetus, Cleanthes, Buddha Gautama, were men whose ideals of self-suppression and communion with God were of no mean order.* I am free to say that there is a marked difference between them all and the Christ, as much as there is a difference between the stoical writings and the Gospel of

* Epictetus (50–135 A.D.) was a Greek Stoic philosopher born into slavery; Cleanthes of Assos (331–232 B.C.) was a Greek Stoic philosopher and boxer; and Buddha Gautama, also known as Siddartha Gautama, was a fifth- or sixth-century wandering ascetic who became the founder of Buddhism in present-day India. These figures share an interest in rigorous self-discipline, as well as an emphasis on philosophy as a way of life, rather than merely a field of study.

St. John. Jesus Christ was a living, breathing, God-in-man personality, linking human son-ship with divine fatherhood. Buddha Gautama, for example, never truly realized his own son-ship with God as to reveal that relationship to man. He strove to pierce the secret of the universe, but never quite succeeded. Then as to reason and faith and the load of doubt—well, if you ask me whether the birth of Jesus Christ was a natural birth or a supernatural one, as an outsider, all I can say is, I don't know, nor does it matter one jot whether it was the one or the other. Similarly, if you ask me whether He did ascend into Heaven with His bodily form, defying the law of gravitation, I say I don't know, nor does it matter. But this I do know, that His life and work and His interpretation of the ways of God with man may so draw one to Him as brother, friend, master, and, through Him, to God as Father, Almighty Sovereign, Benefactor and Guide, and that should be enough for the average man whose object is not arrogantly to question high Heaven, but to make his way thither humbly and piously."

When they arrived at the theater the curtain was just up, and, for a moment, they were engrossed in the simple setting of the play for which Mr. Beerbohm Tree is so remarkable in his Shakespearean representations. In Scene III, where Polonius utters the precept: "Beware of entrance to a quarrel; but, being in, bear't that the opposed may beware of thee," Kwamankra, poking his friend in the rib, whispered, "That is Christian sentiment with a vengeance."

When the curtain next went up, Whitely drew the attention of Kwamankra to a bevy of dark girls with an elderly man, who seemed to be playing the part of chaperone, and who were soon joined by a couple of young men. Kwamankra followed the direction indicated by Whitely, and nearly jumped out of his seat with excitement.

"What is it, Kwamankra?" asked Whitely. "You generally are so cool."

"Pardon me, but the fact is, I must introduce you at once. Those are my friends the Abans, and I am very much mistaken if the young lady at the corner is not Miss Mansa. Come along!" And he literally dragged Whitely after him.

The old gentleman saw the twain coming in their direction, and beamed all over with delight. He was a good-hearted soul, and loved to see the sons of Ethiopia acquit themselves honorably in a strange land, and he had heard nothing but what was good of Kwamankra. The enthusiasm with which Kwamankra was greeted by his friends struck Whitely forcibly, and he did not at all notice the few seconds that passed before he was introduced.

During the interval, Mansa, who hated all crushes, preferred to remain where she was, so Kwamankra fetched her some refreshment, and stayed to talk to her.

"So you deserted us for the Continent without a moment's notice. It was really bad of you, and I hope you have made up your mind now to make full amends."

"Yes, I didn't like the life here," said Mansa. "Somehow it didn't suit me. Besides, I had no friends here, and as my father was going away, I felt I could not stay."

"You must have found Stuttgart congenial, to judge from the length of time you have been away. Your father has been telling me a little about it, and I hoped to hear more from you."

"Oh! that must be another time. See, the curtain is about to rise, and here come trooping in the Abans. You know we arrived only this afternoon by the Dover train, and met the Abans at the hotel; and as they were coming to see Hamlet, my father thought it would be nice for us to come with them."

"Now, that reminds me, by a stroke of ill-luck, I arrived at your hotel the day you left for the Continent half an hour too late, to find the bird had flown."

Mansa felt a little confused; and just then the curtain rose.

The rest of the play interested Kwamankra little, and he was not at all sorry when cheer after cheer called Mr. Tree over and over again before the footlights to receive such an ovation as few artists have received before or since.

"Mind you call before I leave for Africa," said the old gentleman, as Kwamankra and Whitely said good-night.

The friends talked little on their way back to the Temple, and Whitely, divining what was passing in his friend's mind, respected his silence. Before separating for the night, however, Whitely said, "Allow me, Kwamankra, to thank you for giving me such an agreeable evening in such a cultured company.

Your friends, by Jove, are a credit to Africa, and it makes me feel inclined to lead a crusade against narrowness and prejudice."

"Thank you so much. I am glad you think so well of my friends. I hope you will sleep well after all the day's dissipation." This, as Kwamankra showed his friend to his room.

4.

For the next few weeks, Mansa and Kwamankra saw a good deal of one another. From the first, there was a congeniality between the two which went to make all intercourse natural, pleasant, and spontaneous. It was as if they had known one another all their lives; and it seemed the most natural thing that henceforth their joint lives should run in the same tenor. One day, as the twain sat chatting over an afternoon cup of tea, Mansa fetched a letter from a writing-table and, carelessly spreading it out, said:

"I forgot to tell you, when last you were here, that I have been offered the post of headmistress of the junior classes of our home university. I am sure you will be delighted with the idea, for I am going to accept it, and my father agrees with me."

"How can you think of such a thing?" burst out Kwamankra almost indignantly.

His manner was so sudden that Mansa could not possibly control herself.

"Now, what have I done to call for such sharp treatment?" she demanded firmly, yet playfully.

"Forgive me, Mansa, if I have spoken with unwonted heat, only I was thinking—well, I was thinking you might teach me instead."

"What an absurd idea! How can I teach such a big, strapping fellow like you?" said Mansa. "Besides, you are so clever. Surely, you mock me."

"Believe me, my dear child," and there was a slight tremor in the manly voice, "I was never more in earnest in my life."

Mansa seemed puzzled. After a little hesitation, she said:

"You call me 'child,' and yet you would have me believe that I can teach you. Can you be serious?"

"Yes, I am quite serious. 'And a little child shall lead them,'" he quoted. "I was hoping," pursued Kwamankra, "that yours would be the task to teach me the way of duty, and that, when found, you would help me to tread it."

"But how do I know what your duty is? Who can tell better than yourself? Moreover, the gods of our fathers can teach you it, if you need guidance. Don't you know that, Kwamankra?"

"Yes, I know that. But this also I do know, that the gods are wont to make use of human instruments in approaching men. The Infinite finds expression in the finite, and the ideal is realized in the actual. And it has often occurred to me that the childlike hand that shall guide me through life's labyrinthine ways is the self-same one that I now hold tenderly in my own."

She began to understand. She made an effort as if she would withdraw her hand. She hesitated, and the next moment she surrendered the other also.

"You will be my teacher, then?" asked Kwamankra, half-persuasively, half-triumphantly.

"Yes," she simply answered. "So may the gods of our race help me!"

As the days passed, the twain grew in that mutual understanding, the true basis of all happy unions. Now and again he would tell her of his prospects, which he laughingly said were nil, having inherited little else beyond a clear head and a willing heart for work, with which he hoped they would be able to forge their way in life together; to which Mansa would sweetly say that she wished she had a fortune to make things easy, but since she had it not, she would bring him the next best, a loyal heart and true, at which Kwamankra would chide her, and say that was the best of all.

Little by little, Mansa told Kwamankra all that had happened in her little life since the days he knew her as a child of ten.

"You know," she said, talking to him one day, "I often invoked *Nanamu* that I might be permitted to travel to see a little bit of the world, and it seemed they heard me; for soon after, my father took it into his head to visit Europe with me after I had successfully passed my examinations at our university.

When we arrived here, the life of the people seemed to me artificial. Perhaps I could not have expressed my feeling then in those words, but, anyhow, I felt as if I was not in my proper element. Chance took me to Germany. I found things very different there—there, in the Black Forest, I got into direct touch with Nature; the song of the birds, the bleating of the lambs, the fragrance of the fields, all seemed so natural, and I said to myself: Here is my proper place; here the atmosphere wherein my nature may expand. The rest you know. And now, what think you of the result?"

For answer, Kwamankra caressingly drew her nearer to his side.

Summer was waning into autumn, and the chrysanthemum and the sweet mignonette were in bloom, when the lovers decided upon marriage before returning to Africa, where Kwamankra was to start a practice. It was to be a simple affair, at which there were to be no bride's-maids or groom's-men, and only the nearest friends were to be asked. Mansa appeared in church on the wedding day in a simple African costume of her own design, tastefully got up, and when someone asked her the reason for her choice, she said she knew it would please her husband, and, besides, it answered best to her own conception of what was proper. And "so, these were wed," to employ Tennyson's words.

Kwamankra was not long in taking up the duties of life in grim earnest with his dear little wife to cheer and to comfort him. From the first success smiled upon them, either as the result of honest, strenuous effort, coupled with natural ability, or as a mark of the favor of the gods, or both. Gradually they built up a big practice, and by the time their little boy was able to toddle from room to room, and call "Fadder! Mudder!," they had a sweet little home of their own, with plenty of flowers, and sunshine, and love, and God's blessing. Five short, very short, happy years of mutual love and association, and then there came a cloud which, for the moment, seemed to Kwamankra's breaking heart and tearful eyes without the silver lining; for, with the advent of their second born, a sweet baby girl, Mansa, poor wife and mother, paid with her life for that of her child, who, as though she could not stand the gloom she had brought to this once bright home, soon joined her mother, and made the former gloom twice gloomier, and father and son were alone with a twice twofold bond of love between their souls and the souls of those that had gone before.*

And when his little boy of three asked Kwamankra: "Where is 'Mudder?'" or "Where is Sissie?" he would say: "'Mudder' is gone to God, or Sissie is gone to God," as the case might be, and would turn aside his face, lest his little one might know the full extent of their woe.

---

* This sad story recalls that of Casely Hayford's first marriage, to Beatrice Awrakosua Madeline Pinnock, whom he married in Wolverhampton, England, before returning with her to the Gold Coast in 1896. Pinnock was the daughter of a wealthy English merchant and a Fante mother, and was educated first in Accra and then in Wolverhampton. She gave birth to a son, Archibald Casely Hayford, in Axim in 1898, and later to a second son and daughter. The Casely Hayfords' second son lived for only a few days, and Beatrice died of mastitis (then called "breast fever") soon after their daughter Muriel was born. Muriel too then died at nine months old. J. E. Casely Hayford was devastated by these losses, and was said never to have fully recovered. Archibald or "Archie," the little boy referenced here, nonetheless went on to have a distinguished career in law and politics, eventually becoming Ghana's first Minister of Agriculture and Natural Resources under Kwame Nkrumah in 1951.

CHAPTER IV

Love and Death

"'Fadder,' when I was in Heaven, I couldn't come to you; but I could go to 'Mudder.' I was with 'Mudder' in Heaven."

"But why couldn't you come to me?" She hesitated.

"See, 'Fadder,' I have put the pin through," holding up a match-box triumphantly. Then, presently, in baby fashion, taking up the idea—"I was a big girl in Heaven."

"So you were, darling," and he bent down and kissed her tenderly.

Where the bird warbles earliest, and new light
Wakes the first buds of spring; where breezes sleep
Or sigh with pity half the summer night,
While the pale, loving stars look down to weep.
There lies our grave; a slender plot of ground,
'Tis all of earth we own; no cross, no tree,
Nothing to mark it, but a little mound;
But there my darling stays; she waits for me,
The lily in her hand; and when I come,
She will be glad to greet me, and will say,
'Your lily, dearest, gives you welcome home,'
But oh! dear Lord, I hunger with delay;
Tell me, blest Lord, shall I have long to wait?
For I must haste, or she will think me late.

1.

The newborn child opened her eyes upon a mysterious world. In her little face was a puzzled look—a look of half doubt and half knowledge. There was one who seemed to understand the meaning of this doubting expression, and that was the father of the child.

She had come in answer to prayer—in response to the call, long, earnest and pure of motive from mortal to a god, which the gods are wont to answer. Not that the father of the newborn child did not believe in God; but he was sure that in the hierarchy of the heavens, there was order and rule, and, even as the master-mind controlled subordinate intelligences, making them to do and to will of his good pleasure, so did the Father of all, call him *Nyiakropon*, *Zeus*, *Ra*, *Jupiter*, or by what name soever you please, control the powers and dominions of other spheres and the agencies of this world.*

And so it had come to pass that for full twenty changes of the moon he had prayed fervently to the God of Love to visit him in his loneliness, and this child had come in response to that prayer.

But he had also prayed for light, for he knew, according to the teaching of *Nanamu*, the priests and prophets of his tribe, that Love and Light dwelt together in the highest heaven.

---

* This reference to different names for the highest god most immediately refers back to Kwamankra's conversation with Whitely in *Ethiopia Unbound*'s first chapter, but it is also important to note that Casely Hayford's fascination with West African spirituality is a hallmark of his intellectual career. It is most forcefully developed in his 1915 essay *William Waddy Harris the West African Reformer: The Man and His Message*, published as a short book in London. In it, Casely Hayford uses his firsthand experience observing Harris, a proto-Pentecostal Liberian prophet, perform outdoor baptisms in the Gold Coast as a springboard to reflection on the distinctive nature of African Christian leadership in the twentieth century.

2.

To him who saw this vision, the idea of death was familiar. Among his people, at break of day, as men passed one another in the marketplaces, they would greet one another and say, "*Akioo*,"* meaning, hail friend, thou yet livest. And if a man slept and woke no more, they would say he is gone to *Nanamu-Krome*,† and, if he had been a good man, his friends would make libation to him, claiming his protection and guardianship in the ordinary affairs of life.

He had been a father once before—the happy husband of a happy wife in a home where love dwelt; and when death first took the wife and then the newborn babe, he left darkness behind where first was light. It all looked so strange. He only half realized it in the first flush of his sorrow. But as the days wore on, and the old familiar chair by the hearth remained vacant, the darkness in his heart seemed to deepen.

Gradually the light of understanding dawned upon his soul. He came to know that the spiritual side of love was of far greater value than all else beside, and read a spiritual meaning into the offices of love. Sorrow was the path that led him to the innermost shrine where he met God, the *Nyiakropon* of his race, and understood. He could stand by the open grave of his beloved—open, because by spiritual sympathy he could see her as she was—and say: "I kiss these flowers ere I lay them on thy bosom; and when I say 'I,' I do not mean this frail body of mine, which is but a casket. Hear me, beloved! I mean the soul in me, that which can have and has communion with thee, soul with soul, and spirit with spirit, how it does not matter. See, I throw thee a spiritual kiss, and I know thou returnest kiss for kiss, even as of yore." Yes, he had touched the depths of human happiness and the depths of human sorrow, and had come to know that the way to God led from the one to the other.

---

* Good morning.

† Or "nananom kurow mu." Literally, the town of Nanamu.

3.

The physical strain had been too much for Kwamankra. A lurking disease had begun to show dangerous symptoms. A hurried consultation had resulted in the doctors deciding upon an operation. He received the news with wonderful calmness. He rejoiced secretly in the prospect of the unconscious condition of the senses through which he would pass, and hoped against hope that the intelligence of his nature, freed from earthly trammels, might be free to concentrate themselves upon things spiritual, and given a glimpse of the city of the ancient dead of his race, where he was sure his beloved dwelt. It was a wish born of sincere anticipation which flew on the wings of prayer to the Father of Spirits. As he passed off, he was heard to murmur softly the name of his wife, but none knew that, like Jacob of the Hebrews, he had wrestled with God and prevailed.

In another sphere, as if from a dream, Kwamankra awoke, and, though he possessed not his physical body, as it seemed to him, he was sure of his identity as ever he had been. He commanded the full use of his intelligence, and the scene around him, though weird, was by no means unfamiliar. He had the feeling of one who, traveling to a far distant country, and, for the nonce, forgetting the physical aspects of his native land, upon returning, in a moment, recalls the old place again. But it was not without misgiving, as he gradually took in the scene around. It was at the outskirts of the city, not built by men, that he found himself. For walls the city was surrounded by a great lake whose water was as clear as crystal, to attempt to cross which were madness for a mortal without aid.

As Kwamankra stood doubting within himself what he should do, and deploring the presumption which made him wish to encompass knowledge not destined for man, suddenly there appeared before him a being of such untoward mien that he was anxious to fly from his presence, if he only knew how. It had the aspect of a human being, but so distorted were the features, and so woebegone the expression, that he looked to all appearances half man and half beast. Finding no possible way of escape, Kwamankra took courage, and thus addressed himself to the monster: "Sir, I am a mortal from the nether sphere, which men call the earth, and, unbidden, I have sought to catch a glimpse of this glorious city which now I find it were death for mortal to enter unaided. Pardon my presumption, but tell me how I may gain entrance into yonder city, where I may find her whom my soul loveth."

"Thou hast well spoken in that thou hast mentioned the word 'love.' If truly thou art moved by love, then art thou not far from thy quest; and since thou hast uttered the password, I will tell thee the way, which lies in simple trust. Hear me and understand. I was a mortal like unto thyself. I was ambitious and arrogant. I hoped to scale high heaven by knowledge and by the work of man's imagination. I tried and failed, and I am what I am. The gods, in anger, bade me stay here and point to mortals the way to the city beyond, which I may not enter for full thousand summers, as thou measurest time, until my iniquity be purged."

"I do not understand thy speech," said Kwamankra. "If thou art minded to help me, tell me simply how I may cross over the lake, and win my way to the glorious avenues beyond?"

"Did I not tell thee that the way lies in mere trust? I have very little to add. Examine thine own heart, and if there is aught in it that is not sincere and true, thou mayest not enter in."

Then, suddenly, Kwamankra bethought him how in the temples of his native land, he was wont to bow the knee to the God of Love. So, all else forgetting, bending the full force of his will to the task, even on the banks of this impassable lake, he knelt in fervent prayer that he might have courage to cross over. And as he prayed he seemed to enter into a trance, gradually losing consciousness of his immediate surroundings. When he awoke there stood before him a beautiful youth, clothed in a raiment of the fineness of gossamer, which fell in graceful folds about his person. His feet were encased in sandals of crystalline transparency, and his head encircled with a chaplet of lilies of the valley.

Kwamankra was about to speak, but the vision raised his forefinger to his lips in token of silence, and then in a voice full of pathos and sympathy said,

"Mortal! thy prayer to the God of Love and Light hath been heard, and thy homage of love and trust met with favor, and I am bidden to lead thee across into yonder beautiful city; but, remember thou, that it is only so long as thy courage doth not fail, that thou canst safely cross over, that being the bridge over which mortals may enter. But fear not; thy love hath broken asunder the gates of death, and none may bar thy progress."

Thus listening, Kwamankra suddenly found himself walking on the face of the crystal lake, and his companion with him. And when his heart began to fail him, he thought of his beloved, and took courage. Now and again he would seem to be sinking, only to rise again buoyant on the wings of confidence renewed; and soon the crystal lake was passed. There the vision left him, telling him his mission was ended, and he wot not what to do.

4.

While in this state of uncertainty, Kwamankra heard distant echoes of children's voices, so melodious was the strain, and, in harmony, far beyond aught he had ever heard. He strained his senses to hear more, and as the voices drew nearer, he was seized with a sudden wish to behold the beings from whom those sweet cadences proceeded. And that he might see unseen, he hid himself amidst the flowers which grew in rich profusion outside the city walls.

He had hardly done so, when lo! there came trooping past a procession of young children, with palms in their hands, which they waved aloft, as they sang, and the burden of their song was: "Come, let us go to the Father's house; this day he bringeth his children joy; the sun of salvation is setting fast." So sweetly simple were these children, and the only thing striking about them was the purity of their countenances and the lofty grace with which they carried themselves. Kwamankra greatly wondered when he recalled to mind the angelic presence which had a while ago left him. As the procession neared the city, the company seemed to break into little groups, and to disperse in different directions. They played and gamboled and made fun, and, in all, there was nothing fantastic or weird—so intensely human were these children of the air.

In the meanwhile, the keeper of the gate had hied him into the city, even to that part thereof which faces the rising sun, where a goddess dwelt. Thus the keeper of the gate addressed her, bowing low: "Honored among women!* I am bidden by *Nyiakropon*, the father of the gods, to bring thee news of the coming of a mortal into the holy city of *Nanamu*. Since thou art a goddess, thou must know that since thy translation from nether earth, he whom thy woman's heart prizeth above all honor and glory hath constantly set himself to purifying his heart and his ways, if haply he may find the way to thee; and since he is faithful, the constant desire of his heart, forced on the breath of fervent supplications, hath pierced the heaven of heavens and reached the ears of *Nyiakropon*, wherefore it hath been decreed that thou, honored among women, should be the first goddess in *Nanamu-Krome* to receive a mortal who hath won his way to the holy gates. Arise, shake off thy grief, and prepare to receive him whom thy soul loveth."

Him gratefully hearing, the goddess Mansa arose, and commanded the maidens to get all things ready, so that her coming Lord might not feel strange in the city of the immortals. And with music and with frolic did Katsina, her little daughter, superintend all. As for Mansa herself, to the house of praise did she proceed, and, out of the fullness of her heart, did give thanks to *Nyiakropon*. Before the holy altar she knelt, and raising her heart in thanksgiving, the emotion of her heart so overcame her, that she wot not how to begin, or how to end her thanksgiving.

And wherefore was the goddess moved, and whence the emotion of her heart! Scarcely could she veil from memory an earthly scene of unparalleled

---

* This echoes Luke 1:42, when Elizabeth, wife of Zechariah the priest, is filled by the Holy Spirit and declares to Mary, the mother of Jesus, that she is blessed (or honored) among women. Throughout *Ethiopia Unbound*, Casely Hayford suggestively mixes references and imagery from Biblical and Akan theology. In this narrative, Mansa's "firsts" as a goddess parallel Mary's privileged status among women.

pathos and solemnity, as the hour of parting came. It was the last day of the fever which burned out her earthly life. There, in the old familiar chamber, in the home where dwelt love and light and all that she then, untutored, prized dearest in heaven or on earth, stood husband and child—their first born, bone of their bone, flesh of their flesh, so full of promise. She knew her hour had come, and she must needs die, and her little woman's heart rebelled against the decree of the gods. An inward struggle seemed to be going on within her at that critical moment. At last she was heard to ejaculate: "Oh, God, see where stand my husband and my child. I cannot bear to see their grief-stricken faces. If it be Thy will, spare me to them. But, if not, not as I will, but as it seemeth good to Thee."* It was a bitter struggle—this struggle of the heart—if haply it might secure its dearest wish against the decree of heaven. But she was sincere in giving *Nyiakropon* the choice. She had fought and won, and the highest heaven had sealed the victory. Thus the passing away of Mansa. As for Kwamankra, hope ever more sprang up youthful in his heart. Over and over again he found himself wondering whether his beloved was truly dead, or dead only to his physical senses. And, confidence renewed, evermore building upon adamantine foundations, wafted a vow to heaven that his one quest would be to learn the way to her.

5.

"Katsina, mine," said the Goddess Mansa, "I want you to attend to what I am about to say. Ever since you came to me in answer to my tender call, I have taught you that but a thin veil divides *Nanamu-Krome* from the nether world where thy father and brother dwell, and that the veil is drawn, whenever it pleaseth heaven, for converse between immortals and men. This day shalt

* A reference to the Passion of the Christ (Luke 22:42). Jesus asks that the burden (or "cup") of the upcoming crucifixion be taken away from him, but only if his Father wills it so. Mansa thus performs an act of ultimate faithfulness on her deathbed, for which she is rewarded.

thou see thy father, for, even now, he is within the city walls at the main gate. Go, bid him welcome to *Nanamu-Krome*, for I may not go to him yet." Joyously did the maiden saunter forth to do her mother's behest, and, even at the main gate, as she had been forewarned, she met her father, to whom she said, "Hail, father! Mother hath sent me to welcome thee home." At this Kwamankra was startled beyond measure, but, not wishing to betray his bewilderment, he said, "I do not understand, little maid; pray, who may thy mother be, and how knew she that I was here?"

"Do you not know me, father?" said the damsel, half reproachfully. "Mother told me you were coming, and so I ran to meet thee; but how she knew you were here she did not tell me. But, you know, mother is a goddess, and she knows a good many things." The saying surprised Kwamankra, and he turned it over in his mind what it might mean. Was it possible that the devotion and the trust and the love of his girl-wife had blossomed into a personality which was half god and half human even in the nether world? The case of his little girl was easy to understand, for he had caught the import of the words of the poet who wrote:

> "Day after day we think of what she is doing
> In those bright realms of air;
> Year after year, her tender steps pursuing,
> Behold her grown more fair."

Yes, she was fairer than the lilies, brighter than the sunbeams, purer than snow-flakes—his own little Katsina in this realm of light, and yet he had prayed for her return. For a moment he was lost in thought, then suddenly turning to his little girl, he embraced her with all the warmth of a father's heart, and eager to learn all he might of his girl-wife, he said, "Tell me, dear, what may a goddess be like?"

"How funny, father, what am I like? Have I not hands and feet and lips to return kiss for kiss?" And suiting the action to her words, she covered the bent face of Kwamankra with kisses. Even as the homesick traveler, returning to his native shore, suddenly recalls distant echoes of the past, so did Kwamankra begin to catch glimpses and to recall impressions of the sacred abodes of *Nanamu-Krome*. It seemed to him, as if in some bygone age from this self-same abode of the ancient dead, the gods had sent him on an errand to mortals. Even as he thought, the impression deepened in his mind, that one day the gods had said to him: "Kwamankra, this day we send thee forth into the nether sphere to be for us a witness unto the truth; for mortals are ever wont to go away from the truth, whereupon we gods are ready to destroy them. Go, as a thinker among the thoughtless, convince them of their error, proclaim unto them the sovereignty of truth and the eternal majesty of *Nyiakrapon*, the god of truth." It seemed to him that in obedience to this call, he had gone forth, full of courage, full of zeal, resolved to obey the command of the gods; and lo! before his work was half done, here he was, as it were in a dream, back to *Nanamu-Krome*. He shuddered as he thought upon these things, and greatly feared lest he had stirred up the anger of the gods against himself by leaving undone his duty. What would he have to say to his wife upon meeting her this very day!

Meanwhile, his little daughter poured into his ear, child-like fashion, the story of the abodes of the ancient dead. But with all her childish ways, there was something remarkable in the way she put things. A turn or two soon took them to the principal highway of the city of the immortals; and here there burst upon his view a scene which filled him with awe and curiosity. It was simple, yet majestic, ethereal yet earthly; and one feeling uppermost in him was that he had seen the like before in some forgotten age. For a busy, noisy thoroughfare with a multitude of men hurrying hither and thither, here were, as it seemed, a number of peaceful avenues, wearing a beautiful green, like unto moss, which met in one grand broadway. Each avenue was edged with luxuriant shrubs and plants whose leaves showed the most delicate tints of the rainbow in beautiful blend. Here and there lifted their sinewy arms giants of the forest not unlike the cedars of Lebanon. The different walks seemed designed with an eye to quiet contemplation. Now and again the avenues ended abruptly in an ingeniously laid-out garden from which again avenues continued to the broadway. Here and there burst into view magnificent temples. The temples, as Katsina took pains to explain to her father, had been raised by immortal hands, not for prayer, but for praise. A service of praise was just ending, as the twain arrived at the portals of a beautiful temple, and presently the avenues teemed with a moving throng, but with all the congregation, there was neither hurry nor bustle. The men were robed in a kind of loose garment over which was thrown in graceful folds across the left shoulder a raiment of the softest material, crimson in color. They wore sandals on their feet and garlands of red roses and lilies intertwined around their heads. The crimson shade of their apparels showed that they had passed through the narrow gate of sacrifice; the roses in their chaplets were for a token that over the bridge of sorrow they had passed into the joy of *Nanamu-Krome*; and as for the lilies they merely pointed to the truth that humility becometh well the triumphant. Sandals they wore, because they had borne the heat and the burden of the day, for full oft in the Sahara of life they had had occasion to cry:—

Ekwan yi owari, Nyiakropon
Whe bra ma ahedzi yina atsitsiwu,
Na minan aprepra mutu ontu!
Naasu wuada na mayi da wayim,
Ga'm Kwan, Nyiakrapon!

meaning:

The way is long, Nyiakrapon,
Behold the torn and scattered garment,
And the bleeding feet that can scarce move on!
Yet to thee only I may look.
Oh! guide me Nyiakrapon!

One thing struck Kwamankra, and it was this: the teeming multitudes represented every kindred, race, people, and nation under the sun. It was a congregation of select souls, men and women who had humbly done their duty, and done it well, in another life. That was all.

6.

By now the mansion of the Goddess Mansa was within view, and Kwamankra could faintly decipher certain words writ large on the portals. The characters scintillated as if done in living fire; but, upon nearer approach, he noticed that the effect was produced by the silvery beams of a moon-like orb which, by day and by night, gave life and light to the abode of the gods. Thus Kwamankra read:

"Lead thou me on, *Nyami*,
And thou, O Destiny,
Whithersoever thou ordainest,
Unflinching will I follow;
But if from willing heart
I will it not,
Still must I follow!"

He read and pondered, and the more he thought of them, the more he wondered why they were written over the portals of Mansa's place. And while Katsina ever and anon impressed a point, bidding her father note this or that particular temple, even while she was yet warm in her account, they had arrived at the outer court of the mansion, and, saying, "There is mother come to meet us," with a cry of joy and a run, she was in her mother's arms.

"Katsina mine, run into the inner court and quickly set fruit and wine for thy father, for he must be weary after a long journey." So saying, she slipped past the child, and, in a moment, husband and wife were locked in a happy embrace; but even as the panting heart, after long waiting, at last receiving that which it had yearned for, breaks down and cries aloud for joy, so did the twain sob on one another's neck.

"Come, 'tis not seemly for us to give way like this when the gods have been so kind to us, nor must a goddess show weakness in many tears."

"I forget; Katsina told me so," said Kwamankra, starting back.

"How silly of you," said Mansa, "look at me, is there any difference between what I was and what I am, or can aught that may befall thee or me in time or eternity, save neglecting the will of the gods, make me less thy captive, thy bond maiden?"

"'Tis well said. But since thou inquirest, I must own that I see in thee a grandeur of soul, a depth of emotion, that mere mortals do not possess. Yet could I spot thee out among a thousand women. Tell me, art thou in very truth a goddess?"

"Yes, I am a goddess; for *Love* is of *God*, and *God* is *Love*. And so art thou a god, only thy warfare is not yet accomplished. And to this intent was thy prayer heard, and leave accorded thee to visit this sacred abode, that thou mightiest carry hence a knowledge which will aid thee in thy work."

"I can understand you being a goddess, but, surely, you mock me when you suggest that I am a god. Call me a thinker, a teacher, call me anything that is of the earth, but a god I cannot think that I am one, or can ever be."

A look of pain passed o'er the countenance of Mansa as in subdued tones she said: "It is even as it was revealed unto me. Yet another eon must pass over thy head before thou comest to thine own, before thou enablest me to add the finishing touches to thy habitation. All these years I have waited for the fruits of my suggestions, as thy guardian angel, and though thou hast learned much, yet hast thou more to learn, even the lesson of simple trust. A little more doubting on thy part, and thou mightest have lost the chance of seeing my face this day. Yet how my woman's heart hath longed for thee—for a full and a lasting reunion."

"Pardon me, beloved, you talk of trust and seem to sorrow for my want of it. Believe me, I shall learn to trust more. But as for a habitation for me in this city, it is more than I can understand. Have pity on my simplicity, for I am but a mortal."

"I talk of naught, husband mine, that a mortal may not understand. Ever since my translation, I have watched over thee, even as a mother hen watches over her brood. Oft might'st thou have faltered, but that I prayed for thee, and my prayer was heard. Scarcely dost thou rise to the level of thy opportunities. Though a mortal, thou art a thinker, and, even among gods, none may rank higher. By knowledge God planned out the heavens, and laid deep the foundations of the earth. Only thou allowest full oft cold reason to usurp the place of simple trust, and in this thou art harder to learn than a little child. Now, hearken, unless thou becomest as simple and as trusting, eon after eon shall pass o'er thy head before our final reunion."

"It grieveth me to think, dear one, that the time for reunion is with me, and yet I command it not; but think not 'tis willingly done. Tell me, do you mean trust in little things as well as in great, in temporal matters as in matters of higher moment?"

"Yes, my beloved, light beginneth to dawn upon thy soul. Simple trust, remember, honoreth *Nyiakrapon*. Listen! When thou returnest to earth, opportunity will be given thee of preparing in this school, and oh! may'st thou be apt to learn. For our beings must be rounded off, and every phase of our development completed, before translation. And for this purpose are we given opportunity after opportunity until the work of pruning be accomplished. It is all but the finishing touches that are required to thy habitation. Each mortal buildeth for himself a habitation in this sacred place. Some build of stone; some of stubble; unhappy they who raise their hopes upon the shifting sand."

"Yet thou speakest of the finishing touches being put by thee to that which is of my own building. Guardian angel mine, explain!"

"Truly, it is of thine own building. No one may build for another. Even love, such as mine, is helpless in such a case. Come with me, and I will show thee the structure that thou are raising for thyself."

Kwamankra followed, greatly wondering what the full meaning of Mansa's words might be. Close to the mansion of the goddess was rising up a new structure of considerable beauty and strength before which Mansa paused lingeringly.

"Behold," she said, "the symmetry of this building. It is such as displeases not the gods. Yet, if thou perceivest clearly, thou wilt see a seam here, a fissure there, unevenness in places where there should be uniformity. Much as I love you, beloved, I cannot be unmindful of thy imperfections. Reunion may not take place till thou hast laid the apex to a character, fit for a god to dwell in."*

"Once more I fail to understand. How can my character form a dwelling place for a god?"

"'Ye shall be as gods, knowing good and evil,'" quoted Mansa, with sweet emphasis, more to herself than to her husband. Then fixing on him a look of tenderest sympathy, she said, "In the beginning evil and good were created, and to man was given the command to rule and subdue the evil, and to foster and cause the good to prevail. That is the final reason of human experience, and man becomes a god when he has won the victory. It consists in the building of character, and one star may differ from another star in glory. When mortality fails, the immortal in man prevails and finds its home here where, in the cycle of the heavens, in the case of great souls, it becomes a god dwelling in the temple which character hath fashioned. The temple hath truth for foundation, love for superstructure, and child-like trust for apex. Do you now understand, beloved?"

"Yes, guardian angel mine."

"For encouragement," continued she, "beholdest thou yonder rising tower in the structure which thou art raising for thyself whose pinnacle shimmers in the light of heaven?" Kwamankra bowed assent. "That is courage," said the goddess. "It stands somewhat prominently in the edifice, as thou canst see."

"But you puzzle me," said Kwamankra. "I have little courage, as men think of it and preach it. I love not the strife of mortals, neither do I excel in deeds of valor nor of strength wherein, as I understand, the gods delight. I have done no heroic deed in my time that I know of. I have won no battles, led no squadrons triumphantly against the hosts of men."

"Enough," broke in the goddess, with a slight gesture of impatience. "I know you have done none of these things. But wotest thou not as yet that

---

* As discussed in the introduction, Casely Hayford is intimately attuned to the logistical dimensions of Gold Coast state-building. It is notable in this light that Mansa here describes character as a built environment: it will be a *place* for a god to dwell.

I speak not of earthly things, and that, therefore, earthly comparisons are worthless? To love strife, to excel in deeds of nerve, to be leader in campaigns of slaughter—none of these is accounted great or courageous by the Father of the Gods. But to love truth, and to serve under its banner, come what may, that is courage truly, which will endure and stand the test of endless ages." Then turning upon him a look of intensest scrutiny and deepest sympathy, she continued: "Behold, you will stand before kings and princes and mighty ones of the earth to testify against corruption and wrong in high places in the name of truth. Thou hast courage, and the stars in their courses shall aid thee. And now take this message to the sons of men, and I give it thee as an emissary of the gods. Say unto the mighty that the cry of the afflicted and the distressed among the sons of Ethiopia has come up to us, and we will visit the earth. For gold the oppressor will find tinsel, and for precious stone adamantine rock which will fall upon the tinsel and grind it to dust, and the wind will scatter that which is ground unto the four corners of the earth, and men shall see it and wonder at the work of the gods. Lo! *Nyiakrapon* will establish in Ethiopia a kingdom which is different from all other kingdoms. Mammon will have no place therein, and an angel of light, with a two-edged sword, shall guard the gates thereof."

"And in order that thou mightest not falter by the way, when thou returnest to the earth, go to the city beautiful, the mother of the world, unto the part that faceth the setting sun, and thou shalt find a vestal virgin whose altar of love it hath been ordained should be lighted up by thee in incense to the God of Love. Go, she is true; thou hast my leave, and fare thee well!"

"But"—Kwamankra began.

"I know what thou would'st say," put in the goddess. "To obey is our present duty; and remember simple child-like trust is the apex of all—for thee as well as for me. It may be I shall come to thee, if need shall arise. So long as we trust, it will all come right. Go, and again, fare thee well!" And, as an anxious father, watching by the side of a dying wife, restrains the anguish of his heart, lest his little ones might know the full meaning of their woe, even so did Mansa restrain the anguish of her soul before her husband.

"Father, mother says I am to come back to thee in the other world. I wonder if you will know me when I come?" Kwamankra's eyes filled with tears.

"Yes, I will, darling," he simply said.

When Kwamankra awoke, the work-a-day world was going on in its accustomed way, and the old earth still revolved upon its axis in the same duration of time. And the sunlight chased the shadows, and the shadows chased the sunlight, and there seemed to be strife in the elements, but not the strife of mortals. It was effort coordinating with effort, and *Nyiakrapon* ruled over all.

The newborn child opened her eyes upon a mysterious world. In her face was a puzzled look—a look of half doubt and half knowledge. After a few playful years she flitted away. Men talked of a ripe soul. There was one who understood, but said nothing, and that was the father of the child.

CHAPTER V

In the Metropolis of the Gold Coast

In the year of grace, 1904, there was no such thing as a water supply in the town of Sekondi, the pet little preserve of His Majesty's Gold Coast Government. Nor was this in any way strange. The Government and the people of the Gold Coast had always depended upon Providence for such a common necessary of life as water. So, it happened, that when the Metropolis was being laid out into "High Streets" and open spaces, it had not dawned upon the authorities that man was a thirsty animal, and this notwithstanding gentle reminders on the part of experienced men in the past. If you search the Colonial archives, you will find that in the eighties of the old century Dr. Lamprey of the Army Medical Service proposed a simple scheme for supplying the ancient town of Cape Coast with fresh water. The Government went to sleep over the proposal, nor did it wake up over the suggestion to lead the waters of Homo to Accra, the headquarters of the Government. As matters stand, when Providence fails the Metropolis, men are known actually to resort to soda water for the daily ablution.*

Now, if you want to see Sekondi at its best and the water question at its worst, you must approach the town in the month of March on one of Messrs. Elder Dempster's boats, at the season of the year, that is to say, when other parts

* Sanitation and water supply were urgent concerns in J. E. Casely Hayford's Cape Coast, too. Frequent shortages of potable water even contributed to alcohol abuse by the town's young men, as spirits were cheaper and easier to find.

of the country are already being bathed in refreshing showers. As you round off Tacradi Bay,* you see the mother of Gold Coast civilization enveloped in a sheet of overhanging clouds charged with electricity. The side view that is presented shows a city of great promise. Already there are signs of the heavens giving way, and raindrops patter on the ship's deck. But even while you are wondering what a wet landing you are going to have, a blaze of light breaks out on the northeast, and the Titan of the upper sphere leaps forth triumphantly over thunder and storm. As you divest yourself of your mackintosh, a cynical old coaster says to you: "That's Sekondi all over; I shouldn't be surprised if the tanks are all dry."

In other parts of the world harbor works generally precede railways; but here an apology for a pier-head does service for harbor accommodation. The result is you have to land in an open boat often with an angry surf surging around you. Let us assume, however, that you have landed safely. If you had known Sekondi in the days of its pristine innocence, you will find that an iron bridge now spans the ancient natural boundary between the English and the Dutch towns. From the echoes beneath proceeds forth the monotonous dirge of an asthmatic engine which appears to be trying to do the work of two engines in a climate which, according to some, is bad for man, beast, and locomotive.

Where once stood the English town and the uplands beyond, one can see at sunset a number of well-arranged wooden houses on brick pillars, looking quaint and striking in the distance, but disappointing upon nearer view. At the foot of the hill lies the railway station, the first sign of civilization, as you meet it on the Gold Coast. It is the terminus of the "Great North Western" of the Gold Coast. And a beautiful line it is with its sprightly curves and gradients and its thirty-nine miles in something like three hours. But I am anticipating.

If you are not in a hurry to descend, you may come with me to the Manager's bungalow, from the spacious verandah of which you can catch a bird's-eye view of Sekondi, bathed in the twilight, as the sun moves leisurely in the western sky right into the bosom of the mighty ocean. So restful is the scene!

* Now spelled Takoradi.

If you know the history of this town, a momentary sweep of the eye will bring back to memory signs of a former strife; for overlooking the Bay, there stands the old Fort, a symbol of the strife between the Dutch and the English in pre-locomotive days. The struggle, in name, was between two European nations, in reality between two aboriginal factions, who, for aught one knows to the contrary, might have otherwise lived in peace. The Dutch or the English flag was the standard which drew the natives in thousands into opposing camps, and for which they shed their blood freely, only that the white man might obtain freer scope to barter spurious drinks for the precious metal which the torrential rains washed to the very doors of the aborigines.*

It is a sad reflection, but a legitimate one, that in the present day the successors of the leaders, who bore the heat and the burden of the day in order that British commerce might gain a footing on these shores, are not remembered as they should be by the British Government. But it is true that they are protected; it is feared very much protected. To be accurate, they are remembered sometimes in the partitioning of their territories, the minimizing of their authority, and, worse than all, in some cases, in the sowing of those seeds of discord, calculated to destroy the integrity of a people.

The work of destruction, speaking generally, goes on not in the light of day, but, metaphorically, in the dark hours of night. The mighty Titan does not knock down his victim and deprive him of life outright. Oh no! that would be too crude a way. With the gin bottle in the one hand, and the Bible in the other, he urges moral excellence, which, in his heart of hearts, he knows to be impossible of attainment by the African under the circumstances; and when the latter fails, his benevolent protector makes such failure a cause for

* The rivalry between Dutch and English colonial powers, to which Casely Hayford here refers, is especially pertinent to the context of Fante cultural consolidation. Partly in an effort to prevent Asante incursion into coastal affairs, a group of Fante chiefs struck a formal and ill-fated affiliation with the British by entering a formal pact now called the Bond of 1844. For a fuller explanation of its significance, see Joseph Boakye Danquah's essay "The Historical Significance of the Bond of 1844," *Transactions of the Historical Society of Ghana* 3, no. 1 (1957): 3–29, included in "Suggested Further Reading" in this volume.

dismembering his tribe, alienating his lands, appropriating his goods, and sapping the foundations of his authority and institutions. To apply Tennyson's simile, the Titan only knows what the Titan wants, or what he means.* And all the while the eternal verity remains that the natural line of development for the aborigines is racial and national, and that this is the only way to successful European intercourse and enterprise. The situation could not be better hit off than in the suggestive lines of Mr. Guy Eden who, with marvelous insight, has written in the "King of the Blacks":†

> "Clad in the civilised rags of humanity,
> Blear-eyed and shaggy, he limps down the street,
> Grinning about him with childish urbanity,
> Begging of all whom he chances to meet.
> Begging, but not for sound garments to cover him,
> Nor for the food that he longs for, you'd think.
> No, for a civilised passion is over him,
> All that he asks and he craves for is drink!
>
> "But in the days long before the white man appeared,

* Casely Hayford here refers to Lord Alfred Tennyson's 1850 long poem "In Memoriam A.H.H.," written as the poet mourned the sudden death of a close friend and widely considered to be among the most outstanding works of Victorian literature. Tennyson introduces the Titan in the eighth stanza of section CIII of the poem, which reads: "And I myself, who sat apart / And watch'd them, wax'd in every limb; / I felt the thews of Anakim, / The pulses of a Titan's heart." Anakim are biblical giants who inhabited part of the Land of Canaan (located in the Levant region of what is now Lebanon, Syria, Jordan, and Israel), and Titans are pre-Olympian Greek gods. Casely Hayford is thus commenting on how would-be "superhuman" colonial rulers, from their lofty position, rob Africans of the capacity to attain a similar scale of civilizational achievement. Like *Ethiopia Unbound*, "In Memoriam" traverses a wide range of spiritual and philosophical themes organized around a central loss, and may well represent to Casely Hayford the apotheosis of nineteenth-century British imperial literature.

† Little known today, Guy Eden was a late-nineteenth- into early twentieth-century Australian writer and composer who was also, like Casely Hayford, a successful lawyer. His most significant work is a 1907 book of verse called *Bush Ballads*, published in London.

Here on this spot where a town was unknown,
Hunger and thirst were two things Billy never feared,
Round him was plenty, and all was his own.
All was his own, for a tribe paid their court to him,
Called him their King, in those days that are past,
Subjects in scores all their loyalty brought to him,
First amongst men was he then—now, the last!

"Where are all they who would make such a 'bobbery,'
Roaming the bush like glad children at play,
Where the mad whirl of the tribal 'corrobboree,'
Where the wild chaunt at the close of the day?
Scattered and gone, for the world had no room for them,
Far o'er the seas came the pitiless cry:
'Why should they live? Fate has writ large its doom for them,
Land for the whites! Let the black fellows die!'

"'Land for the whites!' Aye, the answer came speedily,
Civilisation, with hot eager stride,
Sweeping upon them with maw gaping greedily,
Swallowed them up in their pitiful pride.
See there the last of them, King in the days of old!
Now 'midst the lowest he takes the last place.
Surely some day, when the story of life is told,
Angels will weep for the last of his race!"

But we were taking a passing view of Sekondi, and our companion was none other than Kwamankra. We have retraced our steps over the railway bridge, and are now in Dutch Sekondi. On the left wing of the street are a number of substantial business houses looking defiantly down upon a small building of four bare walls which represents the Wesleyan tabernacle at Sekondi.

The spot upon which this simple building stands is historic. Here, half a century ago, was waged the civil war between the English and the Dutch, in which the good African missionary, Kwamina Affua, who had been baptized by the good missionaries as James Hayford, sometime British Resident at Kumasi, an ancestor of Kwamankra, and a brother of Kweku Atta, the then Omanhin of Cape Coast, lost his life.* As peacemaker, he had gone to help separate the combatants. In the struggle he was brutally, though perhaps unintentionally, struck down. Peace be to his ashes! It is a sacred spot, and no wonder that the stars in their courses would seem to fight against the powers of mammon in their efforts to dislodge the worshippers.

It being the hour of prayer, Kwamankra followed the crowd into the holy edifice, resolved to see for himself the result of fifty years of missionary effort. He noticed familiar faces here and there. There was Kwesi Yaw, who was quite a kid, and a carpenter's apprentice, in his school days at Cape Coast. How he had aged! The lines of care were thickly marked on his face. Yonder was Esi Maynu, who used to be the laundry maid at the old boarding establishment. Marks of age were upon her too; and when he remembered how gay and sprightly they, the young people, were in those bygone days, a sense of sadness came over him.

What were they doing here? They had come to worship, of course. Did they worship, or did they not, in those far away days when they, the young people, joined hands together in the moonlight under the open sky and sang *Sanko* songs?† Even then, to Kwamankra, the words of their familiar *Sanko* were full of meaning; and as he listened today to the wheezing sound of an old harmonium upon which a missionary boy was performing, he could not help thinking how much his people lost in passing from their ways to those of the white man. For a harmonium they had castanets with which they kept

* As noted in the introduction, James Hayford was J. E. Casely Hayford's grandfather. Kwamankra is here thus an explicitly rather than implicitly autobiographical figure.

† *Sanko* songs (*sankɔndwom*) are sung by members of a group of fisherfolk—such as crewmates or fishermen in the same canoe—bound by a sense of camaraderie.

time as one of their number, Kobina Edu it was, gave the solo of the favorite *Sanko* while they joined in the chorus. He remembered the words so well, and readily recalled them:

Mi sankofu, wo nwhe bra yaku apa,
Inhwe bra wumba arku awiay;
Aryarsa, ye yi wu be biada!
Obiri, Osawu si ay!
Adapawi osawusi,
Mimpona, bada miyamu.
Afi yi na nisini ya funa!
Anapawi, mi dofu, mimpona ba da miyam!

Meaning:

Companions mine, see how well we've struggled,
Behold how far thy children have striven;
If so be, we shall still struggle on!
She is black and comely, she is like unto her sire!
Morning star, thou art like unto thy sire!
My sweetheart, come to my embrace;
My Savior, come to my bosom.
How wearied are we this season!
Morning star, sweetheart mine, beloved, come to my embrace!

How simple, how natural, how spontaneous all this was compared with the refrain of "Dare to be a Daniel," composed and sang by Ira D. Sankey, which the missionary boy, with so much effort, was trying to play in tune. Those were the days of healthy Fante manhood. The nation has missed the promise of her prime, and is likely to bow her gray hairs in sorrow and shame to the grave.

The congregation was composed for the most part of children, clad each in a few fathoms of Manchester homespuns. At the head of the choir was the schoolmaster whose attire certainly invited attention. In his elegantly cut-away black morning coat and beautifully glazed cuffs and collar, not to speak of patent leather shoes, which he kept spotlessly bright by occasionally dusting them with his pocket handkerchief, tucked away in his shirt sleeves, he certainly looked a veritable "swell," but he also did look a veritable fool.*

And this was the sum total of half a century of missionary zeal and effort. Could it be for this that the simple good-hearted fathers of our race had suffered and died? They prayed for light for themselves and for their children's children. But instead of light, say ye Gods, does not darkness brood over the land?

The preacher was a white man, preaching to a black congregation; and outside on the front wall of the holy edifice was to be seen a notice which informed all whom it might concern that there would be a service *for* Europeans in the Club House at the station at a certain hour that day. Kwamankra turned away in disgust.

Later in the day he came across Essi Maynu, the selfsame laundry maid of old days. He said to her: "Do you remember me, Essi?" She looked him up and down, and made a move as if to embrace him, but she checked herself.

"What's the matter," said Kwamankra. "Does your new religion teach you to be shy of old friends? Now, to show you that I, at least, am not changed, I shall come round this evening with some of my *Sankofu*; and shan't we have a nice time with music and with dance?" She raised her eyes in holy horror as much as to say: "Get thee behind me Satan."

Kwamankra retreated like a beaten man; but the lesson was not lost on him. Henceforth he was resolved to devote the rest of his life in bringing back his people to their primitive simplicity and faith. And, in that resolve, he mused upon the words: "Bushido (Shintoism) offers us the ideal of poverty

* Casely Hayford's disdain for Fantes' colonial pretensions as expressed by their English style of dress anticipates that of Kobina Sekyi in his dual English- and Fante-language play *The Blinkards* (1916), one of whose main characters bemoans that he was "born into a world of imitators." See *The Blinkards: A Comedy; and the Anglo-Fanti—a Short Story* (Heinemann, 1997), listed under "Suggested Further Reading" in this volume.

instead of wealth, humility in place of ostentation, reserve instead of reclame, self-sacrifice in place of selfishness, the care of the interest of the State rather than that of the individual. It inspires ardent courage and the refusal to turn back upon the enemy. It looks death calmly in the face, and prefers it to ignominy of any kind. It preaches submission to authority and the sacrifice of all private interests, whether of self or of family, to the common weal. It requires its disciples to submit to a strict physical and mental discipline, develops a martial spirit, and by lauding the virtues of courage, constancy, fortitude, faithfulness, daring, self-restraint, offers an exalted code of moral principles, not only for the man and the warrior, but for men and women in times both of peace and war."

"That is it; that is it; I have it," said Kwamankra. "If my people are to be saved from national and racial death, they must be proved as if by fire—by the practice of a virile religion, not by following emasculated sentimentalities which men shamelessly and slanderously identify with the holy One of God, His son, Jesus Christ."*

* "Virile religion" is Casely Hayford's twist on what is often called Muscular Christianity, a mid-nineteenth-century philosophical and cultural movement that saw masculinity and robust athleticism as intimately connected to the pursuit of Christian ideals. It was especially popular among upper-crust British "public schools"—the social set that Casely Hayford was part of in London—and is associated with the writers Charles Hughes and Charles Kingsley, among others.

CHAPTER VI

The World, the Flesh, and the Devil

1.

For the Rev. Silas Whitely the die was cast. Passing from college to ordination without any fixed ideas as to his own relation to God in his son Jesus Christ, or otherwise, and yielding to the advice of an old college chum, Kennedy Bilcox by name, who at this time was holding the post of Political Officer on the Gold Coast, he had made up his mind to put in an application for the Colonial Chaplaincy at Sekondi rather than continue to face a life of penury as a curate in East London, particularly as he knew a friend or two who would work the back door influence beautifully with the officials at the Colonial Office on his behalf.

"And what is the screw like," eagerly asked Whitely, when Bilcox first made the suggestion to him.

"Oh, it is only a matter of some five hundred a year with an annual rise of twenty-five pounds, until you reach six hundred pounds, besides fees and allowances thrown in here and there, passages in and out free every twelve months, etcetera, etcetera, etcetera, with an assistant chaplain, a black man of course, to save you unnecessary drudgery."

"That is quite good enough for me, minus the etceteras, and I am sure I thank you from the bottom of my heart for giving me an inkling of such a billet. By George! how spoilt you Colonials are; and to think I was going to immure myself in East London for the rest of my natural life!"

"But, remember," put in Bilcox, "you will be subject to discipline. You must not, for example, join the silly band of 'progressives,' or your chances of promotion will be absolutely nil, and you may even run the risk of being shelved altogether. The process of shelving is a simple one. You get down with fever; you are invalided home; you never return again, that is all."

"You needn't fear about that. I have no proclivities that way, but tell me all about the 'progressives' on the Gold Coast."

"Why, they are a mere handful of white fools who are blind enough not to see where their bread is buttered, and who advocate equal rights for the native, and all that sort of tommy rot. Now, between ourselves," breaking out into a low mischievous laugh, "the Lieutenant-Governor himself had progressive leanings when he first came out among us, and would not take the advice of us old coasters. He seemed then as if he could dine off niggers, pardon a bit of Coast slang, until he was bitten, and bitten pretty sharply too, I can tell you. Now he sings the 'progressive' tune no longer," laying particular emphasis on the last sentiment.

"But how was he bitten, and by whom?"

"By the Fantes, of course. Didn't you read in the papers at the time how he was hooted by the Fante women in the central province? I was for bombarding their stronghold and sending the niggers flying all over the country, but the old bounder, the Permanent Secretary at the Colonial Office, who, by the way, is the one who really rules the roost, wouldn't let us. The thing is too bad, to think of niggers hooting a Lieutenant-Governor."

"I confess, Bilcox, I cannot see the magnitude of the offense. I suppose there must have been something to hoot the good Governor for."

"Oh, it was all about the Provincial Council question," answered Bilcox, wearily, as if struck by a sudden thought.* "I must be going home now. My little

* The Provincial Councils being debated here were ultimately established by the colonial Gold Coast Governor Gordon Guggisberg, who occupied that role from 1919 to 1928, as an official governing body whereby Paramount Chiefs cooperated with British colonial administrators. They were controversial in some quarters because they amplified the effects of indirect rule, minimizing the intelligentsia's role in governance and empowering more

daughter will be all eagerness to welcome her papa. I came up to London to draw my pay, and meeting old coasters seems always to arouse the brute part of one somehow."

"How do you mean, Bilcox?" said Whitely. "Surely you must have a better account of your fellows than that."

Bilcox, ignoring the thrust, said in a sad tone: "You know, Whitely, sometimes I cannot stand the funny little questions my little daughter puts to me when I return home from Africa. She has an idea that God has made of one blood all nations to dwell on the face of the earth—you know the quotation; it is more in your line. I don't know whence she got the notion, but, 'papa,' she would jump on my knee, and looking me straight in the face with her delicate blue eyes, 'papa,' she would begin, 'I hope you were very good to those poor African people whom you have to look after. They say they are sometimes badly treated, but you will be kind to them, won't you?' When I am alone, I do think of these things, and my better self whispers to me that the child's sentiments are right, and that they are directly contradictory to my line of official work."

"There is a good deal in what you say. To be frank, Bilcox, I must say I cannot see, for instance, why sensible men should go into hysterics because a Lieutenant-Governor was hooted at. Why, I was at a meeting the other day at the Queen's Hall when Mr. Balfour was hissed at, and for a considerable length of time he could not get a hearing. I don't remember the Hussars being called out to punish the naughty little band of British barbarians, as Grant Allen good-humoredly dubs us. And mind you he was the Prime Minister."

"Perhaps that is the reasonable way of looking at the matter, but we all suffer from an affliction known as Coast conscience, and the powers save you, if you, as parson, should get a touch of it when you get out there. As for myself, I shall go quite crazy one of these days, if I don't soon give up this job."

conservative and compliant "native institutions." For an in-depth history of the Councils' origins and later consolidation, see Kofi Frimpong's essay "The Joint Provincial Council of Paramount Chiefs and the Politics of Independence, 1946–58," *Transactions of the Historical Society of Ghana* 14, no. 1 (1973): 79–91, included in the "Suggested Further Reading" list in this volume.

In due course the Rev. Silas Whitely received his appointment as Colonial Chaplain of Sekondi, nor did he find the emoluments of the office in any way exaggerated by his friend the Political Officer. His mother was satisfied, but to do the reverend gentleman justice, before sailing out, his own heart was full of misgiving first as to his own spiritual condition, secondly as to whether he would have the moral courage, in the face of official stress, to do his duty as a man. A few months of coast life, however, soon settled all his doubts. Why should he worry about the matter of his spiritual condition. He was not the first clergyman who had been troubled with conscientious scruples. He would go through the ordinary routine of his work, and, when his term was ended, he would pack up his traps and go. Besides, it appeared that he had set too high an estimate upon the black character. The blacks, he had come to consider, were nothing but a pack of dishonest people, robbing white traders right and left, smuggling contraband goods, and defrauding His Majesty's Government whenever they could. His duty as a Colonial Chaplain was plain. He must teach these people the elementary principles of honesty, thereby working hand in hand with His Majesty's judges who had arrived at the same result. It was true there were a few exceptions among the educated class, but he was beginning to entertain doubts as to how to place even that class, and he was not at all sure how he would receive Kwamankra even, whom he assured himself he had known just slightly in the 'Varsity, if he happened to meet him on the Gold Coast.

The Assistant Colonial Chaplain was the Rev. Kwaw Baidu, who drew an annual stipend of one hundred and fifty pounds. Besides doing the pastoral work along the railway line, including the management of a mission at Tarkwa, he had the bulk of the chaplaincy work thrown upon him, while the Chaplain himself was content to draw his fat pay and take things easy, as, he took care to explain, the medical officer had advised him to do as little as possible on account of the dreadful climate. Outside purely official duties, the Colonial Chaplain had nothing to do with his assistant, who was a highly cultured man, and, in some respects, his senior, having taken a better degree than the Chaplain. Not that the Chaplain was in any way unkind to the Assistant

Chaplain. Oh, dear no! He only wished it to be mutually understood that between them was a natural gulf fixed—the gulf of a difference in their respective social status. So that if the twain happened to be at work together at the chaplaincy, and the Supervisor of Customs, let us say, called, he would politely say: "Mr. Baidu, would you kindly excuse me, you will find the verandah cool and comfortable," and would never venture upon an introduction.

The Rev. Kwaw Baidu was an humble-minded man, and so long as the Colonial Chaplain did not come in conflict with him upon matters of principle, he did not mind. But, at last, an occasion for stumbling and a rock of offense arose in the shape of the segregation question. The town of Akrokeri had been laid out into a European quarter immediately fronting the railway, and occupying the finest site the neighborhood yielded, while the native chief and his people who by rights should own the whole surface, save such as was actually required for building purposes by the mines, had, with the connivance of the Government, been located on the steeps of a line of hills to the east, for which they had to pay quarterly rent. But when the question of building a cemetery for the interment of Akrokerites arose, and the European inhabitants put forward the view that on no account would they commingle their dead with the dead of "niggers," and the matter was by the Political Officer referred to the chaplaincy for opinion, the Rev. Silas Whitely held that the Europeans were right, and the thing put the Rev. Kwaw Baidu's back up.

"Do you mean to say, you an ambassador of Jesus Christ, that you are going to support any such nonsense as this which knocks the bottom out of all Christian charity? No wonder that the people turn a deaf ear to all my appeals. I will speak plainly to you for once. If you do not yield to reason and the spirit of Christ, whom you and I profess to follow, I will report your conduct to the Bishop, and, if need be, I will appeal to the Archbishop of Canterbury."

"You may do what you like, Mr. Baidu, but you seem to forget that this is a British Colony, and that the salaries of you and me are paid by the Colonial Government, and not by the Archbishop of Canterbury. Besides, I consider your opposition a piece of impertinence, and you must consider yourself suspended until I have recommended your dismissal to headquarters."

In due course the Rev. Kwaw Baidu was compulsorily retired from the Colonial service, and a path, thirty-six feet wide, was marked between the European and native cemeteries, and the former beautifully fenced in with money mostly contributed by the black folk. But the matter got noised abroad, and there wasn't a soul in the diocese of Sekondi that did not come to know of it.

2.

A decrepit old woman, limping heavily on her crutches, made her way into the chaplaincy yard and insisted upon speaking to the white chaplain. The chaplaincy yard was kept scrupulously clean, and the little garden adjacent, with hibiscus and crotons growing in rich profusion, and all bordered with festoons of sweet-peas and scarlet runners in early bloom, showed, as clearly as outside appearances went, that the Rev. Silas Whitely fully appreciated the good things of life.

The Colonial Chaplain had dined well, and was enjoying a Havana under the spreading breadfruit trees which adorned the chaplaincy yard. The full moon threw a spray of silvery light through the myriad leaves of the overspreading branches, casting a halo over his face quite out of keeping with the mundane thoughts which at the moment engaged the mind of the reverend gentleman.

"Yes, I believe in even an ambassador of Christ having a good time. Why should I be such a silly ass as to refuse a whisky and soda at the Club? Besides, we must be all things unto all men. That is clearly the scriptural admonition, and it suits my present humor down to the ground. So there goes it; it is done"—this as he flicked off the live ashes from his cigar.

A deep, low cough arrested the attention of the Rev. Silas Whitely, and he turned to see the direction whence it came. He had thought he was alone.

"Was it you, Nancy?" he said, addressing the old woman. "What brings you here tonight?"

The woman addressed curtsied low. She had been brought up in the Mission school, finishing up in the High School, and spoke English with remarkable fluency. She had loved, and she had· lost—first husband, then an only son who had been unto the husband as the apple of the eye, and, therefore, doubly dear unto her woman's heart. Did I say lost? No, they were not lost. At least thus she had been taught by the missionaries, and when she was sad the chaplain had cheered her with the hope of the resurrection morn. She had come to believe that somewhere, in another sphere, they awaited her; and her one thought was that happy hour, one day, when they would welcome her to a place beside them. She lived for this, and worked for this hope. Now and again she thought she had glimpses of Him who said: "I am the Way, the Truth, and the Life," and she had been told the way to Him was to maintain the truth. A heavy burden, for some time back, had sorely pressed upon her heart, which she felt would be lifted by telling the Rev. Silas Whitely the truth, as she conceived it; and so here she was to do it, and yet did not know how.

A soft wind rustled the luxuriant foliage overhead, and through the branches the bright stars peeped down upon this simple old woman whose only wish was to be in harmony with Nature's God. A sudden inspiration, like the wind blowing where it listeth, came to her. She would tell the chaplain a story, as she had heard he was fond of Fante stories, and was wont to collect them; and what better time than a moonlight night in Africa for telling stories?

Nancy laid aside her crutches, took a low stool offered her by the Chaplain, and cleared her throat of a troublesome cough or two. "I have a nice story to tell you, sir, to add to your collection, and, as I was feeling a little stronger this evening than usual, I thought I would come in."

"Certainly, quite welcome," said the Rev. Silas Whitely. "Fire away, Nancy; I am all eagerness to hear you begin."

"Once upon a time," Nancy began in a clear, sonorous voice, "there went into a far distant country two Mahomedan priests to work for Allah. After a time their paths lay in different districts, and they seldom heard of one another. As was their wont, the missionaries worked in leather and other useful industries; but, as it happened, Akarbah succeeded and grew rich in worldly goods, while Adaku, his friend, merely lived from hand to mouth; yet did Allah bless his labors. As is the way of the world, Akarbah's society was now sought by the highest in the land; and when he counted his beads at the hour of prayer, he failed not to thank Allah for all the good He gave.

"One day as he returned from the house of prayer he met an errand boy, who handed him a bit of parchment, written in Arabic. He opened it, and found it was a message from his brother missionary, who, he knew, was low and humble in the things of this world. 'This day,' so the message ran, 'I, Adaku, thy brother missionary, shall lodge with thee.'

"Akarbah frowned. It was very inconvenient. This very day the High Sheriff was to dine with him, the rich and prosperous Akarbah, and what would he say if he met at his table a mendicant friar of a Mahomedan priest? He was resolved. The thing must not be. 'Here, lad, take this parchment back quickly to my brother Adaku. Make sure and give it to him, and I will give you my blessing and a silver piece upon your return.'

"The lad ran past the camels and the horses and the cattle in the market places, and went out by the fifth gate of the city to find the priest Adaku was not at the place where he expected him to be. Adaku had already entered by the seventh gate, and was already within the holy precincts of the abode of Akarbah.

"'Hail, brother,' was Adaku's salutation. 'May Allah be ever more gracious to thee.'

"For answer Akarbah visibly trembled with agitation. 'Did you not receive the parchment?' Adaku stared vacantly at his friend. 'What parchment?'

"Akarbah gave no answer, but suddenly left the precincts of his abode, as if struck by a sudden thought. The hours passed, but they did not bring Akarbah. At last the truth dawned upon Adaku. 'Evidently I am not wanted here,' and, putting on his sandals and snatching his staff, he passed out of the house of his friend, shaking the dust off his feet as he did so, and never forgetting to mention him, not in anger, it is said, when he counted his beads in the house of Allah."

"What a funny story, Nancy; whatever do you mean?" said the Rev. Silas Whitely, as the old woman finished what she had to say.

"Yes, it is funny," she said; "but you know, chaplain, I have lately had such grave doubts as to whether what you tell us in those beautiful sermons you read out every Sunday about the love of God, of heaven, and the rest of it can all be true; and oh! whatever shall I do after all these years of weary waiting, if they are not true? Where is my husband, and where my son?" and it was painful to see the distress and the anguish in the face of the poor woman.

"Don't go on like that, Nancy. But what is there to make you doubt of heaven and the love of God?"

The old woman dried a tear or two, and said very slowly and deliberately:

"Chaplain, you asked me when I had done telling my story what I meant by it. I have prayed to God night and day for some time to be able to answer that self-same question when it came, and now, God helping me, I will. Know thou, then, that thou art the Akarbah of my story. God hath exalted you above thy fellows that thou mightest be a guide unto us his forlorn little ones, and show us the way of love and the way to heaven. But surely thou hast not dealt in love with thy brother, Kwaw Baidu, who is now out of work, with wife and children depending upon him, whose story is known to all the parishioners for miles and miles around. And oh! if the heaven you have so often preached about hath two ways leading to it, one for us black folk and one for you our masters, what an undesirable place it must be for us after all the weariness here below. But do tell me—you who have raised the hope in me—where is now my husband, and where my child?" ejaculated the poor woman, wringing her hands. "Tell me, for thou hast helped to raise false hopes in me. Oh, God! what shall I do?" and the poor woman swooned away in a dead faint. Every effort was made to revive her, without success, and when the doctor arrived he pronounced life extinct.

CHAPTER VII

Signs of Empire: Loyal Hearts

It was Empire Day—the 24th of May—the day on which was commemorated throughout the Empire the birth of the great white Queen who, in her life, surrounded the British throne with a halo of womanly virtues, the kind of thing before which, in all ages and in all climes, the heart of universal man bows low in reverential homage and respect.*

The Gold Coast is also a component part of the British Empire—as necessary to the complete whole as the smallest link to the complete chain; and so, as the women trooped out this morning in their hundreds in Ethiopian costumes with their hair done up in the most graceful, yet picturesque, fashions, and the children with bunting and palms and flowers, all gay and merry as for a wedding feast, one could easily realize that the heart of the people was true. What could not be made of material such as this—the nucleus of the free Ethiopian Empire that is to be?

Why had they thus turned out? What meaning had "Empire Day" for these simple folk? All they knew was that the great white Queen, the great

* The "great white Queen" referred to here is Queen Victoria, who reigned from 1837 until her death in 1901. In 1876, the British Parliament also voted to name her Empress of India. May 24th was her birthday, which was first celebrated as Empire Day in 1902. Per Casely Hayford's description here, Empire Day was devoted to celebrating Britain's global reach with local parties, concerts, parades, and the like, heralding the central post-Victorian imperial tenets of responsibility, sympathy, duty, and self-sacrifice. At the same time, Casely Hayford invokes such lavish imperial loyalties with a bit of irony.

Awuraba, or mistress, whose son now reigned over them, had been born on this day, and her they delighted to honor; but if you asked them wherefore they loved and cherished her memory, they could not tell you why. Perhaps it was an instinctive feeling that she, a good woman, could never be unkind to them and their people, and sympathy had begotten loyalty. After she was gone, they familiarly referred to her, and said: "*Inde Awuraba niba adzi adzi, wo ma ye nkoko sumunu*," that was to say, "Now our mistress's son reigns; let us go and serve him."

It was a day to be remembered by the merchant, because he lost money by the closure of his factory; by the official, because it gave him a day off and extra drinks; by the school children, because they came in for a treat gratuitously supplied by the simple folk of the community, as a kind of offering to the great white throne. And so it happened that all had enjoyed themselves and made merry.

By Kenny Bilcox this day of days had been spent in looking over the District Record Book for the past six months during which he had been away on furlough. He was to take charge on the morrow, as his assistant was due for leave. But the more he read the more furious did he become. Things had not altogether gone to his liking. It was late in the afternoon; the day had been sultry; and he, faithful servant of the King, had worked late and long. Suddenly, turning round to his orderly: "Kwesi," he said, "run fast, fast, to Mr. Macan and tell him I want him here one time."

"Yes, Sar!" and, in a moment, Kwesi was racing down the main street in the direction of the parade ground.

"Maser want you, sar," said Kwesi to Macan, who was enjoying himself immensely in his own fashion.

"And what on earth does 'maser' want with me on a day like this? Say to 'maser' I dey come."

"Tut! tut! tut! whatever good are you for, I should like to know," said Political Officer Bilcox to his assistant, David Macan, as in return to a low respectful bow, he merely glanced Macan's way in a half nod, half menace. "The fact is," he pursued, "you are too d–m straight for the Gold Coast Diplomatic Service. It is like you Scotch people, you are always putting your confounded conscience before obvious duty. Here you have gone and spoilt a whole eighteen months of strenuous work on my part to put into operation in Insima District the policy mapped out by the Lieutenant-Governor."

David Macan was somewhat taken aback at this sort of reception, and, at first, did not know whether to put it down to the extra rise in the thermometer, extra whiskies and sodas, or to his ill luck in being born with a conscience. Truth to tell, David Macan was a typical Scotchman, as straight as a die, and had already gained for himself among the Africans the sobriquet of "honest David." Reflecting a moment, David said, "Excuse me, sir, but I don't know in the least what you are talking about. Perhaps if you took the matter calmly, I can understand you better. In the meanwhile, let me warn you, sir," his Scotch blood for the nonce getting the better of him, "that much as I respect you, I shall seriously resent the next rash reference you make to my people."

"And what on earth do you mean by allowing that impudent rascal Kwamankra to sneak into this district?" angrily demanded Bilcox, and ignoring Macan's remonstrance. "We'll have our hands full, I can assure you, and you will have to answer for it at headquarters. But whether or not, I won't have you in this district, do you hear? I'll recommend you for leave at once, and when you return, if you ever do, you may go to Kintampor, or some hotter place, for aught I care."

"How absurd you are this evening, Mr. Bilcox, to be sure! How could I prevent Kwamankra coming into the district to practice? Besides, he is a native of the country; the chiefs look up to him; and I had always understood we were to work through the chiefs, and, by parity of reasoning, through their natural leaders."

"Do you call it sound policy to play into the hands of a man who can write such rubbish as this Kwamankra does?" throwing heavily upon the table a thick volume which had been standing on the dirty shelf. "Pray listen to this and tell me whether your senses have fled," this as he read from the open page the following: "'Were there such a thing as political ethics, or a pretense or semblance thereof among Christian nations, as there is a semblance of some sort of Christianity in so-called Christian countries, it might be permissible to inquire how far the conduct of Christian nations in relation to aboriginal races, sometimes charitably called subject races, conformed to the Christian standard of morality—' Now that is rank heresy, teaching the aboriginals that we are a parcel of hypocrites and cut-throats; and to think that the writer of this vile stuff has been let in here through your stupidity!" pursued Bilcox breathlessly.

Macan made a move as if to knock the Political Officer down; but just then a voice from the verandah attracted his attention, and, in a twinkling, Whitely had placed himself between the two.

"There is no reason," said Whitely, "why you two gentlemen should not repair to the back yard and have it out in true sportsmanlike fashion. But as for expressing your opinions of one another freely in the hearing of the black boys, I don't know what to say of it. By George! how they swarmed at the foot of the stairs, peeping one behind the other, until I kicked them off the premises as I came up. Besides, we did the thing differently in my youthful days. Fewer words, you know; but, perhaps, the heat had something to do with it, or I mightn't have had the trouble of interfering," placing himself in pugilistic attitude first toward Bilcox, and then toward Macan. The situation was fast bordering on the ridiculous, and as Macan was in no mood for fun, he snatched up his hat, bowed low, and in a moment he was gone.

"B–oy! b–oy! cocktails, two cocktails, do you hear? and look sharp about it, or by Jove, I will break every bone in your body!" Then turning to Whitely—"The idea of these boys always hanging round and eavesdropping. The worst of it is one can't do without them."

When the servant had placed the drinks on the table and departed, Whitely said: "I would advise you, Bilcox, to be careful what you say in the hearing of these native boys of the man Kwamankra. You have no idea what a hold he has upon the popular imagination, and how widespread is his influence. Personally, there is something irresistible about him I could never withstand. I knew him in my student days. Under normal conditions, I should say it is the charm of a manly purpose and force of character. But, then, no one is normal in these parts." And there was a strange sadness in his voice which Bilcox could not help noticing from the way he laid stress on the words "no one."

"Mind you don't miss the Chief Magistrate's dinner, or he'll never forgive you; the hour is 8 p.m.," said Whitely, as he slowly descended the stairs.

As for Macan, he could not help turning over in his mind the strange medley which was labeled the Gold Coast Diplomatic Service. He remembered reading somewhere before coming out the following: "*It must strike the careful observer that the position of a man in the public service of the Gold Coast is often a difficult one. If such a man is honest and intelligent, he cannot fail soon to discover the peculiar conditions under which he is called upon to discharge his duties. The first thing that will occur to him will be the dog-in-the-manger policy of the Administration, whose servant he is. He will find that, theoretically, the people are free, having their own laws and institutions. He will see that the Government, apparently, recognize this fact; but that in practice, he, the public servant, is expected to interfere with the institutions of the people as far as he dares. Neither is he told to allow the natural development of the institutions of the people, nor is he directed, in so many words, to attempt to mold them. What he does today, which is considered wrong by his superiors, may be done tomorrow by another and applauded.*" As he put two and two together, trying to fathom the real cause of his superior officer's annoyance, the truth gradually dawned upon him. He had acted by the natives as an honest man should do. During the time he had acted as the head of the Diplomatic Service he had given the chiefs every encouragement to unite with one another and to consolidate their authority and jurisdiction over their people.* He had encouraged national schools throughout the district, and supported the Chiefs to make by-laws,

* As we suggest in the introduction, tensions between traditional chiefs and Casely Hayford's foreign-educated, lawyer class of leaders in the Gold Coast were intensifying around the time of *Ethiopia Unbound*'s publication, in large part because British colonial administrators supported chiefly jurisdiction as a way to maintain the imperial status quo. Macan here is coming into awareness of this fact as he contemplates the general hypocrisy of colonial administration, wondering if he has in fact done Kwamankra and other "educated Africans" a disservice by having previously taken his higher-ups at their word.

requiring every child to attend the schools until the age of fourteen. All these were in the line of normal and healthy growth of the people in enlightened progressive ways, and he had worked with a will and a great deal of intelligence and tact. It had never dawned upon him that there was a theoretical policy and a practical one, the latter having as its aim such a shaping of circumstances as would forever make the Ethiopian in his own country a hewer of wood and a drawer of water unto his Caucasian protector and so-called friend. This then was what he was expected to do. Was it right, could he conscientiously do it?

CHAPTER VIII

A Magisterial Function

A splendid repast, in the course of which good spirits and good cheer had flowed freely. The talk had varied from Oxford dons to Japanese admirals and Russian generals; and when it came down to liqueur and coffee everyone was merry, but truly the merriest was the genial host, and a right down good sort he was.

The Chief Magistrate beat himself this evening, and as he waxed more and more eloquent and glibly passed on from one subject to the other, it was only right that the eternal race question should come in for a fair consideration.

They were a body of learned men, the guests of the evening, including the members of the Diplomatic Service, one or two doctors, with a fair sprinkling of colored barristers, and, as it became such a company, they talked learnedly.

"When you come to talk of the jurisdiction of the native Kings and Chiefs I lose all patience with you," said the host, as he wheeled round upon a youthful barrister who had ventured to make an observation upon the destoolment, that is to say, the deposition of the Chief of Agona. "The King of England is King here, and it is ridiculous to think that these little squirts of puppet headmen can be said to have jurisdiction."

Macan of the Diplomatic Service rashly came to the rescue of the youthful barrister. "I thought I had seen such a thing as a Native Jurisdiction Ordinance in the *Corpus Juris* of the Gold Coast."

The host growled and told him plainly, but politely, without much ado, that he knew next to nothing about the matter. Turning to Kwamankra, he pursued, "Now, what do you think—you go up country, and one day one of your puppet kings sends and arrests you and claps you in jail—how would you feel over the matter, eh?"

"At the best of times, I confess," said Kwamankra, "it is not pleasant to find oneself in durance vile. But if the jurisdiction is there, what is there to do but to submit to it?"

"That is exactly what you needn't do. When one of your native authorities comes before me with their confounded jurisdiction notions I treat them as little children, and dismiss the whole thing with a jest. I can assure you, it is a most effective way. Besides, talking seriously, you have not considered the effect of the Order in Council."

"Which Order in Council do you mean?" ventured a precocious full-fledged.

"What else can I mean but the last, which defined the limits of the colony, and vested the jurisdiction in our sovereign Lord the King," almost shrieked out the host.

"My dear sir," put in Kwamankra, "if I may venture to come to the assistance of my young friend, it takes two to make a bargain, as you will find if you examine into the constitutional history of the country."

For the moment the host was nonplussed. He was somewhat hazy as to the historical part of the subject. But as a parting shell, he exclaimed: "Well, be that as it may, it was one of your own men who drew a report upon this very matter upon which the Government have acted. I have seen it with my own eyes, I assure you, and I make you a present of the fact."

"I say, Whitely," continued the Chief Magistrate, "how did you get on with that cemetery controversy of yours? I hear you have given your assistant the sack. I say, it is really too bad of you. I am strong on so-called native jurisdiction, and that kind of thing, but when it comes to segregation of the dead, I tell you the thing beats me. Think of old Lawson, the pioneer of the gold industry, not receiving decent interment on the ground of color. The thing is preposterous, and I am not in sympathy with it." Whitely colored up and appeared confused. The criticism was sharp and unexpected.

The Chief Magistrate was known for his frank expression of opinion, no matter what the subject matter of discussion was. Bilcox thought it was time he came to the rescue of the Government policy.

"Bravo! Chief, I like your fine speech," addressing the Chief Magistrate. "I never knew you were a champion of the non-segregation theory. At the next sitting of the Council I shall not fail to record the considered views of such a highly placed official as your Honor."

"I have never been able to understand the argument in favor of segregation," put in the conscientious Macan unguardedly. "In the time of an epidemic, for instance, I can understand why the afflicted, without distinction, should be put away. But in normal times, to be sure, I don't understand the philosophy of the matter."

"The question has nothing to do with epidemics. The man in the street knows that," sourly retorted Bilcox. "Besides, it is common knowledge that whites never catch small-pox from blacks," he added irrelevantly.

"Ha! ha! ha! ha!" burst out Dr. Castor. "That's good, go one further. In all my experience I declare!"

"You don't mean to insult me, doctor, I hope. Besides, all this discussion before these gentlemen," waving his hand in the direction of the colored fraternity," is most unseemly, and I for one must beg leave to retire."

"Pray, don't go away, Mr. Bilcox," said Kwamankra. "I am sure we are not offended in the slightest. My friends here, like myself, are used to this kind of thing. But what are the odds? I, for one, am strong on *reciprocity*."

"And what has reciprocity to do with this matter?" angrily demanded the Political Officer.

"Only this, sir," began Kwamankra calmly, "that if you took mankind in the aggregate, irrespective of race, and shook them up together, as you would the slips of paper in a jury panel box, you would find after the exercise that the cultured would shake themselves free and come together, and so would the uncouth, the vulgar, and the ignorant; but, of course, you would ignore this law of nature, and, with a wave of the hand, confine the races in separate air-tight compartments. Wherefore I preach *reciprocity*."

"I say, you fellows, we must be going; it is getting late"—this said the senior member of the legal fraternity as he rose, turban in hand, to take leave of the genial host, who was fuming at Bilcox's rudeness. "Good-night, sir, we thank you so much for kind entertainment," he continued, addressing the Chief Magistrate.

"Good-night, gentlemen."

CHAPTER IX

The Yellow Peril

The political wisdom of Ekra Kwow, the son of Kwamankra, was learned at the feet of his father while yet he was in his teens. Being a lad of inquiring mind and quick perception, many a curious question did he put to bis father on odd occasions, when Kwamankra would return answers full of pith and marrow.*

"What is the meaning of the 'yellow peril'?" interrogated the precocious youth, as he craned his neck behind the chair of the paterfamilias, who was leisurely gleaning from the pages of *Public Opinion*.

Kwamankra raised his eyes from the printed matter, and beckoned the young hopeful forward. Eyeing the lad curiously, he said, "If you must know, I suppose I must give you the lesson, and, perhaps, the earlier the better. Now, if you should be going to school to-morrow, and at the street corner Kweku Mensah knocked off your cap and punched your nose, what would you do?"

"I would, of course, punch his head back," answered the lad triumphantly.

"Good! Now let us go a step further. Suppose your school fellows were going on a picnic, and Kobina Tsintsin's boys met you on the public road and barred your progress, would not you brave lads fight your way through?"

"Of course, dad, what else could we do in honor of our school?"

---

* The figure of Ekra Kwow is based on J. E. Casely Hayford's real-life son Archie, with whom he shared a close intellectual relationship. In an unpublished manuscript from 1935, Archie remarks, "We drew such mutual inspiration from our association and the friendship which he extended to me when I was still quite a boy. There was nothing I hid from him and little he hid from me."

"Now, for the application. In geography books you have learned that different nations dwell on the face of the earth—white, yellow, red, brown and black like ourselves. They each occupy a portion of the earth's surface. Those who occupy those tiny islands somewhere in the English Channel are, as you know, called the English. So you have the Japanese, those brave fellows, the Indians, the Africans, or to come down to particulars, among the Africans, say, the Zulus, the Ashantis, and the Fantes. To give the principle which made you punch Kweku Mensah back, and your school fellows bravely break through the ranks of Kobina Tsintsin's boys, a name, let us call it the law of self-preservation. Now, if you relax the practice of this principle in the course of life, you go under, and men then talk of the survivors as the *fittest*, because they have resisted best. You remember those lines in Shakespeare you were reciting to me the other day:

> '. . . . Beware
> Of entrance to a quarrel; but being in,
> Bear't that the opposed may beware of thee—'*

That is a wholesome rule of life, my boy. Well," pursued Kwamankra, "there are certain nations in the world who call themselves Christians, and who claim a monopoly of culture, knowledge and civilization, and who, *ergo*, think that they have a heaven-born right to survive and thrive while all others go under. They are mostly whites, and when either the brown, or the yellow, or the black man resists and shows he does not mean to go under, these self-same white Christian people hysterically cry out: 'The Yellow Peril,' or the 'Black Peril,' as the case may be. Do you understand, my lad?" laying his hand slowly on the child's head, and looking him straight in the face, so that the child's eyes met the father's fully and meaningly.

* Polonius speaks these famous lines to his son Laertes in act1, scene 3 of *Hamlet*, telling him to avoid fights whenever possible, but to make sure his opponent fears him if he must enter one.

"Yes, I do, dad," replied the lad. "But tell me, dad, I did not wish to interrupt you before—why did you call the Japs, 'those brave fellows?'"

"Why, simply because in the present contest they are engaged in with Russia, they have shown they do not mean to go under, whoever else may do so; and they have caused the cry of 'the yellow peril' of late to go up more hysterically than ever.* Listen to this rare bit," said Kwamankra, reaching for his scrap album and turning to the letter J: "The sacred duty is incumbent upon us, as the leading state of Asiatic progress to stretch a helping hand to China, India, and Korea, to all the Asiatics who have confidence in us, and who are capable of civilization. As their more powerful friend, we desire them all to be free from the yoke which Europe has placed upon them, and that they may hereby prove to the world that the Orient is capable of measuring swords with the Occident on any field of battle." These words were spoken in the Japanese House of Peers, and they embody the principle I have been trying to inculcate upon you in a nutshell. You will do well to remember them all your life; and since I find you an apt pupil likely to pass the lessons on to others after I am gone, I will tell you of my experiences with the Political Officer."

"But what is a Political Officer?" queried the stripling.

"There you are again with your inquiring little brain. I must begin from premises to conclusion, step by step, like the *quod erat demonstrandum*† you were worrying me with the other day. Still you are right, my boy. Once define clearly, and all difficulties vanish, as mist before the noon-day sun. Well, the system of Government under which we, the people of the Gold Coast, live is known as the 'Crown Colony system.' It is a system somewhat behind

* Probably a reference to the Russo-Japanese War, fought by the Russian and Japanese Empires in 1904–1905 over their rival ambitions for Asian territorial expansion. Japan's victory secured its role as a major global power, and Russia's defeat was among the most prominent factors leading to the First Russian Revolution of 1905.

† A Latin phrase, "what was to be demonstrated." It can be used at the end of an argument to show that the argument has been proven and is complete.

the times.* Now, what would you boys think of your schoolmaster in these enlightened days if he should, from time to time, ask you to contribute out of your pocket money funds for the laying out of a recreation ground without allowing some of you boys to have a say as to how things were to be done, and what games were to be bought for the school? I am sure you would all revolt and say, 'If you are going to use our money, you might at least let us say what games we would like.' Under the system I am telling you of the schoolmaster is the Governor, and the lads are the people of this country whose contributions are in the shape of the heavy duties they pay on all imported articles. But they have no voice in the spending of their contributions, and that is why I say the system is somewhat behind the times. To proceed, seeing there must be discontent among the people, the Political Officer is the man appointed to deal with cases arising out of such discontent."

"But how? I don't quite understand, dad. Does he go and speak kindly to the people and tell them not to mind, and that they will have the value of their contributions, if they are patient?"

Kwamankra burst out hilariously, and for some minutes could not control himself. The lad began to feel sheepish, and thought he must have said something very odd. But, presently Kwamankra came to, and a look of sadness seemed to play upon his countenance as slowly he murmured to himself the words:

"and its heart as pure as now."

Quick as thought, memory had flashed back that unique chapter in his life's experience when she and he had watched over this very child in infant slumbers, bone of their bone, flesh of their flesh, and in the fullness of their hearts the prayer had gone up:

---

* Crown colonies were distinct from other forms of overseas British administration—such as dominions, territories, or protectorates—because they were under the direct authority of the crown, via a governor. They neither possessed their own representative government nor were represented in Britain's Parliament.

"That when time's mystic fingers wrote manhood
on its brow,
Its deeds might be as gentle and its heart as
pure as now."*

And now, he was left alone to help realize that prayer in the youthful enquirer. Mastering his feelings, and, for the moment rolling a stone over the sepulcher of the ever virgin past, Kwamankra turned to his son, and drawing him closely to his heart, spoke gently thus: "How I wish I could keep you, my boy, from knowing the seamy side of life. But since knowledge must come some day, it were well I guided thee to the sources thereof, if so be it might not be all gall to thy thirsty soul.

"No, the Political Officer does not exactly do what one should think, my boy. Here on the Gold Coast the people have also shown that they do not mean to go under, but in a different way. You know the story of the wolf and the lamb. I see you are all eagerness. Well, it will bear repetition. The wolf meets the lamb on a thirsty day by a stream. The wolf stands higher up the stream and drinks, while the lamb quenches its thirst in the lower part. Presently Mr. Wolf says to Master Lamb, 'what do you mean by making the stream muddy?' 'How can that be?' says Master Lamb, 'since you are higher up the stream than I am.' 'I hear you spoke disrespectfully of me three months ago,' puts in Mr. Wolf. Master Lamb meekly: 'I have been in the world only two months gone.' 'Well, if it wasn't you,' replies the wolf, 'it must have been your father who did.'"†

* Casely Hayford seems here to be quoting from memory a poem by Burlington B. Wale, "The Dream of Life," published in an 1849 book called *The Heart's Memories, Or Records of Perished Things*. The couplet's correct lyrics are: "That when Time's mystic fingers wrote manhood on its brow, / Its deeds might be as guileless—and its heart as pure as now."

† This is a tale from Aesop's collection of fables. It has variations across different cultures that speak to the same lesson: oppressors can easily find ways of legitimizing their unjust behavior. The proverb at the beginning of Jean de la Fontaine's version of this fable, for instance, may be translated as "might makes right."

"Coward!" cried Ekra Kwow, excitedly. "Don't I wish I were close by with my little pop gun? I should have put a hole through Mr. Wolf right enough."

"Good, my boy, that's well said. But, unfortunately, it is an everyday occurrence in this world, and, what is worse, we can't always bring to play our pop guns when we may morally be justified in doing so.

"But it is high time you were in bed. Another time, if you are good, I will tell you all about the Political Officer, and my experiences with him, if you remind me how far we have come today."

"Good-night, dad!"

"Good-night, my boy," and, in a minute, he had disappeared behind the curtains, leaving Kwamankra to his thoughts and to his pipe.

CHAPTER X

The Black Peril

"Here, on the Gold Coast, the people have shown that they do not mean to go under, but in a different way—" this, as the precocious youth produced a sheet of paper with the words neatly written down. "I meant not to forfeit the rest of the story you see, dad, and now for your promise please," drawing a low seat close to the paternal chair.

"I see you have forgotten the illustration but not the text, and as other illustrations are easy to find," said Kwamankra, "I shall redeem my promise. They are scattered over the pages of history. In your historical lessons you have undoubtedly heard of what is called the 'Eastern Question?'"

"Yes, I have, though I forget what it was exactly, and, besides, I learn these things better when you tell them to me your way, dad," said the lad excitedly.

"Now, if you will compose yourself, and remember that the story is in illustration of the discussion with which we started, namely, the so-called 'yellow peril,' you will listen to good purpose, my boy."

The youth bowed assent, and Kwamankra began: "It was all the doing of the Russians at the start. Years ago they were confined in one corner of Asia Minor, having no access to the North Sea, the Baltic, or the Black Sea. By-and-by the Emperor, Peter the Great, conceived the idea of Russian expansion toward the Crimea and northward to the Baltic. After him Catherine II of Russia sought to carry into effect the dream of Peter the Great, and thenceforth it became the national policy of the Russian Bear."

"What do you mean by the Russian Bear?"

"It means the Russian in the sense in which we talk of John Bull."*

"Oh! go on dad."

"Well, in the pursuit of this policy by the Russian Bear, she came in collision with the Turk in the Crimea about the time of the Emperor Nicolas II in the fifties of the last century; and a *casus belli* (of course you have been brushing up your Latin) was found in the fact, and I wish you to note this particularly, that the Turks ill-treated the Christians of the Greek Church within the Sultan's dominions. You perceive the application of the story of the wolf and the lamb here, don't you?" The youth gave a knowing bow. "Well," pursued Kwamankra, "it is a long story; but, in the act of self-preservation by the Turks, although history recordeth it not in so many words, the circumstance constituted in the minds of the Russians of the time a 'Muslim peril,' do you understand?"

"Yes, dad," answered the youth eagerly. "But, surely, the English people have never acted thus toward a weaker race. I can well understand the sneaking bear thus acting, but not straightforward John Bull."

"Well, let us see, I am not so sure about that. What of the Opium War with China when England coerced China because she insisted upon restricting the sale of opium within the Chinese Empire, and the 'Lorcha Arrow' incident not so many generations ago, where England picked a quarrel with China, because Governor Yen exercised the right of boarding a Chinese vessel which wrongly flew an English flag to cover her piratical practices in Chinese waters?† Other instances might be given, but I can assure you, my dear boy, no

* John Bull is a fictional personification of the United Kingdom, rather like France's Marianne or America's Uncle Sam. The character of John Bull has satirical origins but later came to be seen as a symbol of freedom and bravery. He is depicted as an "ordinary" Englishman: fleshy, sensible, and down to earth. That is why Ekra Kwow describes him as "straightforward John Bull." The writer, who does not believe that the English have been fair in their dealings with "weaker" races, is being ironic when he refers to the positive qualities attributed to John Bull.

† The British won the First Opium War against China (1839–1842). The Second Opium War, also known as the Arrow War, broke out when Chinese officials seized a ship called the *Arrow* in October 1856. As Kwamankra mentions, the ship was stopped on suspicion of piracy and was flying a British flag. Britain, alongside France, Russia, and America, used the

Christian European nation is free from the error of self-assertiveness—none free from the taunt of crying 'yellow peril,' or 'black peril,' the moment they are confronted with resistance in one form or another. They seem to carry in the one hand a patent from the Almighty and absolution in the other to snatch away the patrimony of others:

> 'Why should they live—Fate has writ large its doom for them.
> 'Land for the whites! Let the black fellows die!'

the European nations seem to shout, and reck not offense to God or man in the cry."

"But how does all this apply to our country?" asked Ekra Kwow.

"How does it?—good! I like to think you are following so closely what the learned books call the argument, that is, the immediate subject under discussion. Well, I will tell you in one word. The Political Officer represents the self-assertiveness of the English in extending power and authority at every nook and corner wherever the thin end of the wedge can be introduced. The sagacious black man offers a point of resistance when he pleads his peculiar customs and institutions, and presto! the cry of the 'educated native peril' is raised, as if forsooth, the 'native' ceases to be a 'native' the moment he is educated. The genuine cry might be 'the black peril,' but that won't do at present. The wolf and the lamb story again, you see."

"But why don't you expose these things, dad? You can write, you can talk, why don't you let the whole world know of them," said the lad with some degree of heat.

"Not so fast, my boy," said Kwamankra, laying his hand on the child's head, and speaking slowly and deliberately, as was his wont when about to

---

incident as an excuse to wage another war against the Qing Empire, who lost the second war in 1860. At the end of each Opium War, the British implemented treaties in their own favor, such as the legalization of opium, the establishment of ports for Western trade, or the free movement of Christian missionaries. A lorcha is a kind of boat.

give vent to some utterance from the very recesses of his soul. "I wish you to understand, my dear child, that it is neither the anger of the powerful, nor the hope of favor from the great that has hitherto sealed my lips. I have taught you from your infancy to regard truth as the highest of all virtues, as the apex of character; and he who falls in declaring the truth in his day and generation, is but a humble follower of a Socrates, or if you prefer it, of the Nazarene. I try to follow his example, prepared to suffer if needs be in the cause of country, race, and humanity," and drawing the child nearer, he added in suppressed tones—"only the hour is not yet come. Pray for thy father, that when it does come, he may be found strong and faithful."

CHAPTER XI

On "The Great North Western"

"I say, boys, what class are you traveling," shouted Aban to Tandor-Kuma and Kwamankra.

"I go neither first nor second," returned Tandor-Kuma; and as the Gold Coast Government Railway boasts of only two classes, Kwamankra said, "Look here, you fellows, I am a man of peace. If you are going to have any larks, I would rather take the down train twenty-four hours hence."

By this time the bell announcing the hour for the departure of the train had sounded. So Kwamankra rushed to secure a first-class ticket, leaving the "Professor" and Tandor-Kuma to their own devices. When he returned, the two had occupied seats in the first-class compartment and started to make themselves merry with the good things which Kwamankra had provided for the journey.

"Here's to you and another five hundred a year, as the chaps over the water say"—this as the "Professor" raised his glass in the direction of Kwamankra. Seeing there was no alternative, the latter resigned himself to the situation, and good-humoredly toasted the company round.

"Teekets! teekeets!" shouted the collector from the second-class end of the "composite carriage." Of course, you know what a "composite carriage" is? If you don't, I will enlighten you. It is the kind of thing on this particular railway in which the whites travel at one end, their servants and the black élite at the other end, while the ordinary blacks are packed like sardines in a detached carriage, labeled "second-class." Not that there is any rule prohibiting black gentlemen from using a first-class carriage, but the fact is the class referred to know better, and have too much self-respect to travel first, except on rare occasions when they can have a carriage all to themselves.

To resume, "teekeets! teekeets!" sounded nearer. By this time the "Professor" was in the middle of a Mississippi story, and his brush with buffaloes and other hair-breadth escapes. After taking a cheap degree, with his usual erratic disposition, Aban had been traveling, often supporting himself by odd jobs, and had included in his experiences an acquaintance with the Japs of whom he was never tired of speaking. The ticket collector eyed the three black gentlemen furtively once or twice, and seemed to have come to a mental resolve not to disturb them for the nonce, nor did the trio disturb him by so much as a momentary notice of his presence.

Just as he was about retreating to the second-class compartment, Kwamankra shouted after him, "I say, collector, won't you have a drink?" holding out to him some whisky and soda—"the others do it, you know," and this with a knowing wink.

The collector was human. He hesitated, then made up his mind, took the drink, and went away. Presently he returned and became communicative.

"I don't know, Sar, if any of you, Sar, be lawyer man, Sar?"

Tandor-Kuma chuckled. "What next," demanded the "Professor" sternly. Kwamankra held his peace, appearing not to listen.

"I don't know, Sar, but I bin tink say I da go show you di rules which say di collector mus examin ebery gentman him teekeet."

Kwamankra began to fumble in his pockets.

"My good man," said the "Professor" to the collector, "I have made it a rule never to give up my ticket on *this* line till I have landed safely at my destination, do you understand?"

The emphasis seemed to upset the equilibrium of the collector. He sneaked away, may be, to reflect upon the advantage of an emphasis, and sure enough, he was soon heard letting off steam in the second-class compartment at the expense of an inoffensive Fante.

By this time the train had passed Mansu. Shortly after leaving that station there was some trouble with one of the vans getting off the rails; and it was a matter of half an hour before it was set right. Halfway between Mansu and Ashieme, some timber was taken, and as they steamed away in the twilight, the train with its composite appendages was a full furlong long! Soon they were in thick darkness.

"Light, collector, light!"—this from Kwamankra, for in the detached carriage could be heard yells and shrieks of women and children.

"I say, collector, light! Do you hear? Light!" and this with an expletive or two from the "Professor." The expletive did its work. The collector made his way to the composite carriage amid a scene of much confusion.

"You had better go and fetch the Inspector to see about this mess, or I will report the whole lot of you fellows, white and black alike. It is perfectly disgraceful, this kind of thing," said Tandor-Kuma.

The Inspector, who had, in the meantime, been hurried to the detached compartment by the shrieks of the women and children, had by this time got into the composite carriage.

"What the deuce are you doing not having yet lighted the carriage," he said to the collector with an offended air.

"I no get mach, Sar! Railway no buy me mach, Sar!"

The Inspector made as if he would knock the collector down, but thought better of the matter, and, snatching a borrowed match box, quickly tried to light the lamp. Puff! went out the light.

"Try again, Sir," suggested Kwamankra dryly. "There may be a drop of water in the oil." Puff! went out the light the second time.

"Try again! try again!" came from all sides. "Shall I get out and buy you some paraffin, Mr. Inspector? You know this is perfectly disgraceful. Thirteen shillings for thirty-nine miles and no oil," said Tandor-Kuma.

"Try again! try again! knock him down, teach him a lesson," shouted some roughs. It was getting a bit exciting. The Inspector beat a hasty retreat.

"They call dis di Govmont railway. It is di dirtiest hole I have been in. South Africa, East Africa, North Africa, they be countries. Dis country is disgraceful to the British Govmont," put in a Frenchman at the corner.

Pu! pu! pu! piyu!! Pu! pu! piyu!! came the heartbreaking snort from the nostrils of the iron horse. It reminded one of an overworked omnibus horse at midnight in Oxford Street. First backward, then downward, up the incline, and down the gradient, toyed the iron horse, and as Tandor-Kuma thought of his wife and children waiting dinner in the cozy little room across the bridge, he could not help inwardly bestowing a blessing upon the devil and all his works. It was not until 9:30 p.m. that the terminus was made, the party having left on their 39 miles run at 2:30 p.m. As the trio walked the lonely streets, where black men are scarcely seen after sunset, the Professor, as a parting reminder, said to Kwamankra, "On principle I never pay for a ticket on this line until I have made the terminus, and if you are a wise man, you will take my tip."

CHAPTER XII

A Leader of Society

Tom Palmer, the son of Jonathan Palmer, of Horse Road, Ussher Town, Accra, was a goodly youth of many fine qualities. The Palmers originally hailed from Sierra Leone, settling on the Gold Coast early in the fifties of the last century. By dint of great energy, combined with uncommon business tact, the first Palmer had gradually won for himself a competence which the second Palmer, with equal tact, had gone on improving, so that when it came to the turn of Jonathan Palmer, he was looked up to as a man of wealth, position, and influence in the community of Accra.

Jonathan Palmer had contented himself with moneymaking, but his son and heir, the goodly Tom Palmer, had combined book learning with his other accomplishments, and gone to the extent of taking the L.Th. degree at the College in Freetown,* though he never had the intention of entering the Church. He was fond of controversy, and as the L.Th. course combined a certain amount of historical information, he had followed it so as to be able to hold his own against all comers, as he pugilistically put it. For a calling he had chosen agriculture, and was an expert in the secrets of soils, manures, and seasons. Not that he practiced agriculture, as men practice medicine for example. Oh, dear no! He was a dilettante and no more. It was enough for him

* Casely Hayford also attended Fourah Bay College in Freetown, Sierra Leone, a city that was known in the colonial period as the "Athens of Africa" on account of its reputation as West Africa's premier educational and cultural destination. Founded by Anglicans in 1827, Fourah Bay's list of illustrious alumni also includes Samuel Ajayi Crowther, an influential Nigerian intellectual and freed slave who was West Africa's first African Anglican bishop.

to be able to say with truth, I am a scientific agriculturist, and I can give you a point or two. Besides, in a community like Accra, where every respectable citizen has a calling, it would not have done to appear a loafer.

Tom Palmer was an ambitious youth. His aim in life was to be the leader of society in the community where it had pleased Providence to place his father and his father's father before him. His was the family fortune by right after the pater was gone. He would be the leader of the black aristocracy. What was there to prevent it? And, so, he set to work with a will. The cut of his coat was always up to date, and, on the Sabbath, he studiously appeared in church in a silk hat and patent leather boots, and never forgot his button-hole and gloves of approved style, though he was never guilty of the solecism of wearing the latter by reason of the tropical temperature. For the same reason also he generally wore his coat sleeves a little turned up, so as to show plenty of linen, and the tips of his trousers followed suit, so that you could count the white buttons on his boots. Other youths of his generation looked on admiringly—looked on, and pined, and strove to be like him in appearance, and many succeeded, though they had not Tom Palmer's culture, for which his early associations were responsible, or his money.

Freetown is an advanced African community. Notwithstanding the fact that some, not having the fear of God in their hearts, have thought it fit to malign her in print, still the reader may take it from the writer that it is a community that has nothing to be ashamed of. It has produced many a distinguished citizen, remarkable alike for intellectual attainments as for business enterprise and success, so much so, that Her late Majesty had thought it not amiss to bestow the honor of knighthood upon one of her esteemed sons. Besides, the city boasts of a cathedral, a rarity in the West African Dependencies. The singing is one of the finest on the West Coast, and men like Canon Spain, Canon Wilson, and Canon Moore, all black clerics, would do honor to any English See. It was no wonder, therefore, that Tom Palmer was truly proud of his Alma Mater, the Fourah Bay College, duly affiliated to Durham University, and of the City of Freetown, the Mecca of West Africa. Truly, if there was one thing more than another for which

Tom Palmer revered the memory of his paternal grandfather, it was the utter unselfishness with which he had transmitted the savings of his father before him to his son Jonathan, and the likelihood of the latter obeying the paternal injunction to transmit, in his turn, the family fortune to the next generation, that is, to him, Tom Palmer. Yet, for all that, he could not quite forgive his great forebear for quitting the thriving community by the banks of the Roquelle at the time he did.

With all the lightness of manner we have seen in the subject of this sketch, yet must it be placed to his credit that he was generally most careful when taking any important step in life; and to all the vexed questions in West African social life, perhaps to none had he given such close study as the marriage one. For, mark you, Tom Palmer's aim in life was to be the leader of society, the *wankora wonkor*, as a Fante would say, in social life at headquarters. Yet he could not make up his mind somehow to do the thing. He had discussed the matter several times with friends without ever coming to a satisfactory issue, and it was, therefore, with particular relish that in conversation with Kwamankra one day, who was at Accra about this time for the Agricultural Show, he managed to introduce his favorite theme. Nor can we blame him. Every young man contemplating marriage does it. He worries everyone he meets upon the subject upon the slightest encouragement, until finally he makes a fool of himself, or escapes by the skin of his teeth.

With an old world complaint upon her lips, the master philosopher met the complainant with the hint that one thing, after all, was essential. We all know the story, but some have, perhaps, not noted the human side of it. The complainant was plainly jealous of the marked attention the master philosopher paid to the younger sister. Her womanly instinct told her that the latter was fast discovering "the one thing needful." Her self-love asserted itself in the request, "Bid her that she help me." A charwoman's aid would have been as good. But, truth to tell, she would herself sit at the great man's feet, if she only knew how. It may be, thoughts like these were passing through Kwamankra's mind, as he slowly repeated more to himself than to his companion, the words of the teacher: “But one thing is needful!” then somewhat abruptly turning to the young man he said, “You are making the same mistake that most of us have made. We seem to think that love only comes when she is wooed in Parisian skirts and Regent Street high heels. Know then, my friend, that spiritual sympathy, like the wind, comes we know not whence. Happy the discerning ones who recognize the Queen of Heaven in whatever guise she approaches the waiting soul.”

The young man was puzzled. He spoke his thoughts aloud. “What has all this to do with what I heard you muttering about the one thing needful?”

“What to do with it? I should think it has all to do with it,” said Kwamankra gravely. “You have read the story, I daresay. The master finds a haven, a restful place, in the home of this particular family. Sympathy springs up between him and her who loved to sit at his feet, drinking in, as a thirsty soul, every word that fell from his lips. Interpret the master’s sentiment as you may. But there is no need to disguise the fact that Mary had found the secret of life.”

“But then, all this is beside the question, if you will permit me to say so. The sympathy between Christ and Mary was a thing apart, a spiritual relationship, if I may so put it. How can you talk of it in the same breath with mundane matters—with the vulgar thing which men profess and affect,” said Tom Palmer, warming up to the subject in a way that interested his companion greatly.

Kwamankra eyed the young man for a second or two, and then said with a slight tremor in his voice, “If Jesus was not truly mundane, he would have no interest for you and me. Besides, if you knew of the gift of the gods, you would not speak of love in the way you have done. At one time I was of like mind as you are, but riper experience has taught me that there is nothing vulgar in love, and that the feeling, in whatever guise it exhibits itself, will be found, in its last analysis, to be the self-same thing, and remember then, that where love is, there God is. Great love, great soul! As the streams flow into the rivers, and the rivers into the sea, and yet the sea is not full, even so does universal sympathy, from the cooing of the dove to the fervent heat of a Romeo, find its diapason in the God of Love.”

"I must confess," said the young man, "that this way of looking at the matter is altogether new to me. But am I to understand that you would find excuse for the kind of sympathy that flies off at a tangent here, there, and everywhere?"

"I will state you a stranger proposition then," said Kwamankra quietly. "Remember, my young friend, to begin with, that love is a spiritual magnetic force, and as I showed at the beginning of our talk, like the wind it bloweth where it listeth. Remember also that there are affinities and repulsions where one might least expect.* Oftentimes one starts from the north pole, another from the south, and the magnetic force draws them on and on until they meet, and, in this sense, are we the children of circumstances. Now, think of it. Here is a man of great magnetic force, evoking sympathy and love wherever he goes. But he is a mere man. The corresponding force which he attracts and calls into play here and there becomes created entities, begging for life and claiming the right to live. Tell me, what is the duty of the giver of this life, under God, or to put it materially, the creator of this force? Must he allow free scope to the play of sympathy, or must be ruthlessly set to work to destroy the hope of *light* which he bids spring up in a human soul?"

* Casely Hayford's language of magnetism and forces here draws on the teachings of Theosophy, a nineteenth-century esoteric spiritualist movement with a large following among Victorian and post-Victorian intellectuals. The movement was founded in New York City by a Russian emigré mystic and writer named Helena or "Madame" Blavatsky, who had been inspired by her travels in Tibet and India to form and espouse what she called a "synthesis of science, religion, and philosophy." Casely Hayford's introduction to Theosophy came by way of his son Archie, then a student at Cambridge, and he enthusiastically attended Theosophy lectures in London. The first West African Theosophy study group was founded in Nigeria in 1908, and the region's first full Theosophy lodge was established in Accra in 1935. Though Casely Hayford died too soon to become a member, he had developed a close friendship with the Accra lodge's founder, a teacher named Kwao Brakatu Ateko, at what was then the Prince of Wales College at Achimota (now Achimota School). Blavatsky's most famous work, and that which Casely Hayford is therefore most likely to have read, is *The Secret Doctrine*, published in 1888. See *The Secret Doctrine*, ed. Michael Gomes (New York: TarcherPerigree Publishers, 2009), listed under the "Suggested Further Reading" list in this volume.

"Again, I do not understand you, unless you would imply nothing material in what you say."

"I have said nothing that is difficult to understand," pursued Kwamankra. "Bear in mind I am speaking of true love. I am not referring to a mere wild senseless passion, the result of egoism, the kind of thing which finds satisfaction in multiplying wives, and, from that point of view, I speak of things spiritual rather than material. This, then, I say that no one who has the capacity to evoke sympathy in the human soul has the right ruthlessly to quench the fire once his flame has kindled. I will tell you a story, if you care to listen."

"Go on, please," said the young man.

"Well, here it is. 'Once upon a time there lived a youth who in the heyday of joyous inexperience, as he chanced by a certain out-of-the-way village, evoked love in the breast of a young damsel much below him in degree, and he wot not the full meaning of what he had done. The years rolled leisurely past, and her lover never returned. In the meanwhile, he had become great, gotten himself honor and riches, and, withal, love besides, as he thought. Now and again in the dim recesses of memory a recollection of the maiden would come back to him; but he would say, that is a thing of the past, let the dead past bury its dead. But, as obeying some irresistible impulse, day by day, the thought gained upon him. What was at first a mere curiosity to know what had become of her, grew in intensity until it ended in a regular quest. Abroad he bade his servants go, if, haply, some news might come of her for whom his soul panted. But no news came. At last he gave up hope, and seemed to take no delight in his goodly surroundings, nay, not even in his wife, nor in his children and his home. One day, outside the city gate, as he returned from a lonely walk, he saw walking toward him the self-same woman whom youthful inexperience turned not back to see. Their eyes met. They had both aged so. They had also suffered. She frankly put forth her hands. His touched hers. "At last!" she exclaimed, "my woman's heart told me sooner or later we should meet again." "and mine has been long lonely without thee," he said. "Moreover, riper knowledge has taught me that in the kingdom of love, nothing is ever lost."'"

The story ended, the teller paused for a second, and then added, "Maybe you will now see in a truer light the one thing needful which shall not be taken away from her."

"Now putting philosophy aside for the moment, I daresay you have flirted a little in your time," said Kwamankra, good-humoredly, then, with a mischievous twinkle, "and you may have a child, a poor nameless one, in some out-of-the-way corner of the world. You needn't be shy about it. All of us do do it, though not all of us are men enough to own it.* Now, believe me, my friend, any child of Eve, who has deliberately become the mother of your child is worthy of your love, and to treat her as an outcast is to be unworthy of the name of a man. In this wise, we pagans are more Christ-like than so-called Christians. 'He that is without sin among you, let him first cast a stone at her. And again, He stooped down and wrote on the ground,'" he quoted somewhat irrelevantly, then continued: "In Africa, she is protected; she is a wife. Call it polygamy, if you like. In so-called Christian countries she is despised, a prostitute, a leper."

In the fullness of time, Tom Palmer got married. None of his wives sought to be a leader of society, and he was well content. He himself did not seem likely, now that he had come to his heritage, that he would fulfill the promise of his early ambition. In due course the little ones came—so gladsome their little black faces wherever they appeared, the fulfillment of the radiant love which gave them birth. And as the years rolled by, it was sure that his girls were growing up to be useful members of the community, for Tom Palmer

* Kwamankra's call for generosity toward children born out of wedlock, as well as their mothers, here reflects Casely Hayford's own complicated family life. While he only had two official wives, he fathered children with nine women: Lucy Abadoo, Beatrice Pinnock, Adelaide Smith, Awura Brew, Princess Amissah, Sophia Cobalt, Nonoh from Cape Coast, Christina Hayford, and Patience Johnson.

had made up his mind that he would have no Parisian skirts or Regent Street high-heeled nonsense, as he bluntly put it, nor would he ever condescend to explain himself.

CHAPTER XIII

Reaping the Whirlwind

Tandor-Kuma lay sick with malaria. The fast boat that should have borne him to the bosom of his family had come and gone. In his dreams he had been talking wildly, and asking when the boat would be in.

It was not without reason that his uppermost thoughts seemed to hover about the movements of the steamers. There was in this house where he lay stricken, as a nurse, the mother of his first child—the kind of child the world sneers at and elects to ignore, who, nevertheless, thrives and prospers to the amazement of those who talk glibly of the inscrutable ways of Providence.

He had hoped that in the few days he had to spend upon the business which brought him down, he would be so occupied and pressed with engagements, that he could very well manage to evade meeting more than in a casual way the mother of his child. And now a fortnight must elapse before he would be well enough to travel, and during that time what was to happen?

It is an unpleasant truth that in the first flush of the shame of the mother of his child, instead of bearing up bravely and sharing the shame with her, like the coward man that he was, he had gone so far as to protest that he was not the father of the child, and had allowed her alone to pass through the valley of humiliation; but the God whom she had wronged, according to the theologians, had not suffered her to be entirely crushed. Meanwhile, Tandor-Kuma had succeeded in life, mounted up steadily in his calling, been happily married, and was a most respectable member of society. To do him justice, he was absolutely true to his wife, whom he loved, and never meant to be otherwise. In fact the contrast between his early escapades and his present constancy and devotion to his family was the common talk of those who had known him in early life.

And here was he, after all these years, confronted with the same forbidden fruit of his early days. He was young and full of fire in those days, it is true. He had fallen then. Was it likely he could resist now that he began to feel the same old witchery taking possession of his heart, and making a fool of him, if not in deed, in very intention? "O, God!" he cried, ardently and sincerely, "save me from this." But even while he cried, another voice within him said, "What does it matter? Is it your fault that you are stranded here?"

In the domestic arrangements of a West African home there is hardly any system; and so it happens that the master or mistress orders about the nearest hand available. This was a kind of hospital home. What was more natural than that Ekuba should gradually work her way to the bedside of him whom her heart adored? When the fever had abated a bit, now and again she would steal in with some daintily prepared refreshment which she would coax the patient to partake of. She would often stay to say a word and to smooth his pillows. On such occasions Tandor-Kuma would seem ill at ease, and appear as if struggling with some inward emotion.

Careful nursing had brought Tandor-Kuma back to health; but, as it sometimes happens in West Africa, the boat that was to take the convalescent home had not turned up according to the timetable, and time was hanging most painfully on his hands; and every day the Titan of sheer sympathy was tightening its grasp stronger and stronger round his heart, leaving his senses reeling.

One evening Ekuba came to clear away the supper and found Tandor-Kuma sitting at a corner of the room reading, the others having gone to a Fante concert. She boldly drew a chair, and sat down near him.

"What a jolly thing your steamer delaying like this. Supposing she did not come for another week or so, I wonder whatever will happen?" Tandor-Kuma raised up a finger deprecatingly.

"I know," continued Ekuba, not heeding the warning one little bit, "that you are dying to get back to the bosom of your dear family—that is what they call it, isn't it? but what must be, must be."

"What do you mean, Ekuba, you talk rather strangely tonight."

"I simply mean this, that I have missed you badly all these years, and now that the spirits of my fathers have thrown you in my way once more, surely you will not begrudge me a little of your society. I took a job here with your kinsman, the doctor, feeling sure you would one day turn up."

"Don't talk like that, Ekuba. You know I must be careful. I am a married man, and I must think of my wife and children."

"If it comes to that," she said, "I am your first wife, and the second is an interloper." So saying, she burst out into a wild laugh. The situation was becoming perilous and yet comical, and Tandor-Kuma could not restrain a laugh too. Here he was with the woman, who first raised sympathy in him, confronting him with a naïveté that was quite unusual. Should he repulse her? He quickly decided that the wisest course was to humor her and talk the matter out in a half-bantering, half-serious way with her.

"You know," said Ekuba, taking advantage of a momentary pause on the part of Tandor-Kuma, "the last time you were here, and you had to go away so suddenly, when I came and found you were gone, I was so sorry," looking at Tandor-Kuma defiantly.

"Were you? I am not surprised. You see we all make mistakes in life, and we are expected to pull ourselves together and go straight after. If not, often the last stage is worse than the first. You don't wish to see me down, do you?"

"It depends upon what you mean by seeing you down. Kobina had to come, and nothing could prevent it; and I have waited all these years," repeating the last words with a slow emphasis and a weariness of tone which struck Tandor-Kuma awkwardly.

"If you talk like that, I shall never come to this place again, when I go away this time."

"It doesn't matter; I shall wait; and it may be some sudden business or family matter will bring you down."

Tandor-Kuma revolved in his mind how to meet this flank move. Meanwhile she continued: "You know I go to chapel? Last night the minister told us in his address that, once upon a time, there was a king who was in the habit of killing his subjects for no good reason. One day he sent for a parson. The good man feared and wondered whatever was going to happen. He made excuses, but eventually had to go. While going he broke his leg. It took some days to set him right, and he was well enough to continue his journey. When he arrived at the king's palace, he was dead, and so the parson was saved." She stopped short, eyeing the man she loved feverishly.

"Well?" interrogated Tandor-Kuma.

"Well, simply this that what must be must be, and what must not be must not be—that is the rule of the gods"—pointing her little chin up triumphantly. "And after all," she went on, "was it such a grave error? You know the murderer was not saved, but the thief was."

"But what if the thief went on stealing," retorted Tandor-Kuma. "It is like going against the light."

"Light, then darkness," Ekuba put in with a far away look in her eyes.

"Yes, but when the light comes, then darkness goes away," suggested Tandor-Kuma.

It was all very fine, this toying with fine phrases and sentiments when passion answered to passion in the breasts of two human beings. Ekuba lapsed into silence, and it was evident that both man and woman were struggling with the same inward emotion.

"But tell me," Tandor-Kuma incautiously broke out, "what made you run away from me the last time I was here before I got married."

"How simple you men are? I ran away from you? It was not so. I simply went to avoid compromising you in any way."

Tandor-Kuma would have liked a little time to reflect. But suddenly Ekuba swept away the supper things, and, in a moment, she was gone.

The next morning, a gentle tap was heard at the door of Tandor-Kuma, and a voice from within said, "come in." Ekuba boldly entered, and placing down some clean linen, flung herself at Tandor-Kuma's feet, who was already dressed and reclining in a low chair by the open window. Tandor-Kuma got up and faced her.

"What is this you have done," he said under his breath, perceiving the awkwardness of the situation. For answer Ekuba got up and deliberately locked the door upon the outside world. Then facing the man, she said, "Tandor-Kuma, these many years my heart has hungered for your sympathy, and now that the gods have brought you back to me, surely, you will not deny me one kind word. Just say you care for me a little. That is all I want."

Tandor-Kuma made a move as if he would unbolt the door. In that instant Ekuba held him spell-bound with a look so pitiful, so imploring, so passionate that he quailed before her gaze. He hesitated, then wavered. The next moment he completely broke down. Erring love had conquered, that was all.

CHAPTER XIV

The Black Man's Burden

A bamboo shanty, doing service as a Methodist place of worship at the end of a "High Street," with a mud house roofed with corrugated iron, doing service for Belial,* with gin shops and sheds studded all along the line at short intervals at the other end—such is a typical scene in a well-known growing African community in the neighborhood of the thriving mines on the Gold Coast railway. It is a terrible scourge, a veritable canker, eating its way slowly, yet surely, into the very vitals of the life of the black people among whom this plague of modern civilization is planted.

It is the Christian Sabbath and the hour of morning service. Ding, dong! ding, dong! goes the bell, calling the devotional black folk of the community to worship. They are not inattentive to the call, if one may judge from the group after group of men, women, and children wending their way up the little rising on whose summit stands the House of God. The women far outnumber the men, and the house is filled to its utmost capacity. At a corner, all by himself, sits a son of Albion,† a man of independent character, the butt of the camp, who dares to worship with the black folk on this holy day. It is a motley gathering of all conditions of men in all sorts of costumes from the latest Regent Street cutaway coat to the ample four fathoms of Manchester calico print, gracefully wound round the person. At 10:30 of the clock there mounts the pulpit a black parson who, from that hour till 11:50, reads Psalms and Litanies and hymns to the melody

* Another word in the Bible for the devil or Satan.

† Another term for Great Britain.

of an inharmonious portable American organ. No wonder half the congregation go to sleep, and the beadles have their work cut out for the rest of the morning. One of their number, aggravated by the extra rise in the thermometer, is a bit aggressive, and no wonder that a distinct unchristian scowl is clear on the face of a Christian gentleman sitting next to the observer.

Meanwhile, the reverend seigneur is discoursing in an unknown tongue to the majority of the congregation for all he is worth, and when he condescends at length to render the sermon into the vernacular, the finest Job-type in the congregation is not listening, but wondering when this labyrinth of a service will end. In the meanwhile, what of the house of Belial?

"Pretty polly! pretty polly! how do do? Quite well, thank you, pretty polly! tut! tut!" are the various sounds that attract the attention of the wayfaring man from the throats of half-a-dozen tropical birds attached to the house of Belial. It is true the worshippers are but few and far between, mostly, and, in fact, nearly all, of one race. But their worship is real, sincere, and earnest. The black folk are beginning to understand and to appreciate that there is other worship than that of God, and that both are taught by the white man's fetish which they call civilization.

But a livelier scene remains yet to be described. The inmates of the gin shops are issuing forth in their tens and larger groups. They dance and gesticulate, as if seized by some evil spirit, and the uproar is worthy the confusion and the clamor of the nether regions. That is also the white man's work.

And so it happens that the black man along the line is sorely pressed by a threefold burden—the burden of allurement in the shape of gin drinking; allurement in the shape of houses of ill-fame; the bantering hypocrisy of the allurer. Heavens! what curse is equal unto this curse!

Meanwhile, from the Moslem quarter of the village community at dawn, noon, and dusk goes forth the voice of the Muezzin, as from the minarets of Mecca, calling unto the faithful to prayer. They drink neither wine nor strong drinks, nor suffer them to come near their habitations the unclean thing. They keep alive their primitive simplicity and faith, combining Godliness with contentment. It is a struggle between the Cross and the Crescent. Which will win? It looks as if the Crescent will win in the end, judging by the Divine standard of life; and yet Christ is stronger than Mahomet. But the House of Christ is divided against itself, because the men of that House, nay, the very leaders and the lamp bearers, are untrue!

"Good evening, Sir," said a white miner to Kwamankra. "Can you tell me where the West Indian gentleman who plays the guitar lives?"

"Certainly; if you will step over here I will show you," said Kwamankra, rising up from his simple evening repast. "You know the market place; if you will walk straight down and take the first turning to your left, I believe you will find him in the first house but one."

Kwamankra settled down to his meal, thankful to have got rid of what threatened to be a serious interruption to his thoughts.

In ten minutes the miner came back. "May I come in?" he asked.

"Yes, do," replied Kwamankra.

"I did not find him; they say he has gone down to the Coast. What is your name?" essayed the miner; "you speak English so well. Are you a lawyer?" He spoke a little thickly. Kwamankra did not answer, but put on a whimsical look which said as nearly as possible, "what if I am?" at the same time beckoning the miner to take a seat.

"You know I have seen you somewhere before. Your face is familiar. It must have been on the train," persisted the miner.

"Yes, I come up and down here pretty often."

"You know I came down tonight on purpose to have a little fun with the photographer over the way. I am good for a right down American singsong, and, if you don't mind, we can have a fine time together."

"No, thank you, I have some writing work to do, and I must be getting on before bedtime. Kofi, please show this gentleman round to the photographer's across the way"—addressing his servant on the verandah.

"Oh, may I have a drink of water?"

"I have some Tuborg beer, excellent stuff; perhaps you will find that pleasanter—Kofi, fetch some beer." The miner subsided into the comfortable canvas chair round the corner.

"Well, Boss," he pursued, "I know of a little job I can put in your way. There is a man in my camp who has worked for one year and fourteen days, and just because he had a little fun today, he has been turned adrift, and he is to pay his passage back home. Now, do you think that's fair? If you will take up the matter, I will send him round in the morning. What name shall I say?" The same quizzical look and a smile by way of encouragement to get on and be finished with the business was all the response Kwamankra gave.

Meanwhile, the miner drained his second glass of Tuborg beer. He grew more confiding. "You know," he said, "they want me up there to do a platelayer's work; but old B. insists upon paying me only fifteen bob a day, and, as I am no fool, I keep my '*sabi*'* there," pointing significantly to his head. "Besides, they think I am too familiar with the black people, and when they see me sitting down and drinking with them, they don't like it; but I don't care. There is no part of this district I have not been to, and the Fantes have always behaved to me like gentlemen, and I am always ready to do them a good turn. Yon know old B. wanted to play me the same trick as my pal. He says to me the other day, 'You are drunk, and, if this occurs again, away you go bag and baggage.' Mind you, I wasn't drunk. Today I got drunk, and I go up and says to him: 'Now, Mr. B., I am drunk, and very drunk too, and if you are a man come out in your shirt sleeves, and we shall have it out.' He was as tame as a lamb"—this almost in a whisper, accompanied by a low laugh. Kwamankra joined in it heartily.

"Kofi, show this gentleman the way to the photographer's—mind you, Sir, there are ditches in the way," said Kwamankra.

"Good-night, Sir," returned the miner. In another ten minutes he had returned. Kwamankra was busy with his scribbling. He hardly dared interrupt the flow of ideas.

"The photographer is out, I am told," explained the miner.

* West African Pidgin English for "knowledge." A pidgin is a simplified language that develops when people from two or more groups must interact over an extended period but do not have a language in common. It is composed of elements from the different languages.

"Very good, Sir—good night," said Kwamankra, hardly looking up from his writing.

"As a last favor, would you mind showing me where I can find a bed for the night? I am told there is a hotel about here."

"I am sure I don't know of one, and I would advise you to get back to your camp," said Kwamankra, fixing a penetrating glance upon the miner, which said plainly, "I wonder if you are an honest man." With this the miner vanished into the outer darkness, but the story is silent the while whether the same operation was not repeated elsewhere that night.

The next day Kwamankra was due down the Coast, and he took the afternoon train with the "Professor" for a companion. The second-class compartment was full, so they traveled first, and though there were many angry glances, none dared question them. Kennedy Bilcox, the Political Officer, was also going down by the same train, and being minded to be gracious, and having had an extra parting glass more than was good for him, he was inclined to be confiding. Besides, though he immensely disliked men of color, he judged it politic outwardly to be on the best of terms with the leaders of the people. He thought he gained their confidence that way. Rather he raised their suspicions, and was accordingly mistrusted.

On this auspicious occasion, he was full of the big things he had done up country—how he had metaphorically thrashed the Chief of Tandosu into humility, and how he crouched before him with fear, poor man! Presently he turned to Kwamankra and said: "I say, do you know that rascal Kobina Bua? I hear he is your client. You had better advise him to behave properly in future, or, by Jove, he will find himself at St. Jago."*

"But what has he done?" queried Kwamankra.

"What has he done! Why the fool is perpetually drunk, has lost all sense of decency, and is always making a 'palaver' at Tandosu."

* Fort St. Jago, located in Elmina in Ghana's Central region, has served different roles since its construction in the sixteenth century. Over the centuries, it has been a chapel, a military base, and a prison.

"Oh, is that all?" said Kwamankra, provokingly.

"You do surprise me, Mr. Kwamankra. To think that a man of your position and education should see nothing to condemn in the disgraceful conduct of Kobina Bua!"

"Personally I condemn no man, but since you talk of condemnation, permit me to point out to you that the greater condemnation lies at the door of the Government whom you represent, and whose servant you are. You condemn Kobina Bua, and you presume to do so by reason of the fact that you are a Political Officer. As a fair-minded man, let me invite you to look at the other side of the picture. You know that trade gin contains fusel oil and other deadly noxious ingredients. You also know that that is the stuff the Government permit to be imported into the country and which eventually finds its way down the throats of 'rascals' like Kobina Bua. You dare not stop the importation of the vile stuff. Why! Because it would affect salaries and pensions and duty allowances and other perquisites. In the name of reason, how can you expect the average black man having the means to indulge in gin drinking to keep his head and behave decently? And so when a Government Officer pays a visit to one of these otherwise harmless African dignitaries, and he is received by the latter with extra warmth, whereupon the Officer losing his self-control, vents upon him his wrath in eloquent periphrasis and damning reports reach headquarters, the observer, if he is a seeker after truth, certainly feels tempted to tap the Officer lightly on the back and say: 'Thou hypocrite, first cast the beam out of thine eye, and then shalt thou see clearly to cast the mote out of thy brother's eye.'" Kennedy Bilcox appeared thunderstruck, but Kwamankra, unheeding, continued: "You know, and the whole world knows, that if the black chief and his people stopped consuming the vile stuff the merchants offer them, the whole machinery of Government would stop running for want of the necessary grease. You are a Christian, of course. When you meet your friends, and, in conclave, you are inclined to be hard on my client, remind yourselves of the Master's saying: 'Ye make clean the outside of the cup and platter . . . ye tithe mint and rue and all manner of herbs and pass over judgment and the love of God.'"

As the Professor and Kwamankra shook hands at the station, the former said to his friend: "Those were brave words. But you may be sure this kind of thing will get you into trouble one of these days. But here's my hand on it, whenever you need help I am your man."

Kwamankra spoke low: "I have counted the cost, and, it may be, I shall need thy help when the hour comes."

CHAPTER XV

As in a Glass Darkly

Not so very long ago in the age of the world, the Nations were gathered in council upon Mount Atlas, even at the point which is nearest the ancient city of Constantine, and there were no people that were not represented, save the Ethiopians, whose kingdoms stretch from the shores of the Mediterranean, where it washes the Lybian coast, across the great desert, taking in the arms of the mighty waste from ocean to ocean, thence sweeping down to the remotest parts of the provinces inhabited by the Kaffirs, a race of mighty men.*

It was like the meeting of the gods, the gathering of the Nations, for they had mastered all knowledge and gotten themselves such power as to make men forget the Power beyond, before whom the Nations of the Earth are as grasshoppers.

These Nations, who, in the old pagan days, struggled the one against the other in true manly fashion, had learned a new method of warfare, which they labeled "Diplomacy"; and when the uninitiated asked the reason for the change, it was explained that it was dictated by the spirit of their common religion which inculcated universal brotherhood, and the beating of swords into plowshares. Wherefore it came to pass, that at this universal conference the Nations said smooth things to one another which no one believed.

* Casely Hayford is metaphorically describing the Berlin Conference of 1884, which is often seen as the official start to the Scramble for Africa, or the Partition of Africa. The "gods" referred to here are the European nations who met to determine the division and colonization of the African continent.

But there was one thing concerning which these mighty men were in earnest, and that was the capture of the soul of Ethiopia. Said they, "We have all increased in knowledge and power, and, being brothers, we can no longer devour one another. Yet must we live. Taught by the instinct of self-preservation, we must have elbow-room wherein our children and our children's children may thrive. Now, before our hosts lieth the whole stretch of Ethiopia from sea to sea. Come, let us partition it among ourselves." They were well agreed upon this matter, but not upon the way of encompassing it.

One Nation said, "How shall we do this thing, seeing we are Christians?" Another said, "Thou that doubtest, thou art merely slow of counsel. This thing is easily done. We shall go to the Ethiopians, and shall teach them our religion, and that will make them ours, body and soul—lands, goods, and all, for all time." and the saying pleased them all.

It came to pass upon the third year after the meeting of the Nations that a mighty prince, sailing from the setting sun, dropped anchor in that portion of Ethiopia which is washed by the waters of the Gulf of Guinea. Retinue he had none, nor arms, nor any outward sign of power. In his hand he held a simple cross, and gifts besides. The Sons of Night gathered around him in great awe, and took the coming of the stranger for the visit of a god. But the gifts set them easy, and the drink of the white man was like nectar unto them.

There were discerning men among the Ethiopians who would shake their heads and say, This thing will bring us no good. But the crowd submitted to the worship of the new god, and greedily devoured the good things found upon his altars. And soon the discerning ones formed themselves into a group, and the crowd in another camp; and the thing pleased the strange visitor. And now he sent over the seas, and brought yet other teachers, who apparently taught the self-same doctrine, and the more they taught the more the people broke into smaller groups, each denouncing thẹ other heartily. And so it came to pass, that children who had suckled at the same breast and had played with the same toy gods were, as men, feign to slay one another. And the thing seemed to please the newcomers, and, being men of knowledge, they winked at one another and said the rest would follow.

By this time the unthinking crowd were beside themselves in emulation of the white man's ways, and when they bowed the knee in the House of Mammon, they thought they worshipped the true God, and seemed to forget that once they were Ethiopians.

The gods met in the ethereal heights of Mount Atlas to undo the work of mortals. Said they, "The Nations are as a dream before us, and they know not what they do. Are not the Ethiopians a peculiar people, destined for a peculiar part in the world's work? An end to the machinations of men!"

In the self-same era a god descended upon earth to teach the Ethiopians anew the *way of life*. He came not in thunder, or with great sound, but in the garb of a humble teacher, a John the Baptist among his brethren, preaching racial and national salvation. From land to land, and from shore to shore, his message was the self-same one, which, interpreted in the language of the Christ, was: *What shall it profit a race if it shall gain the whole world and lose its own soul?*

CHAPTER XVI

Race Emancipation—General Considerations: Edward Wilmot Blyden

The year 1907 found Kwamankra at Hampton, in the United States of America, as the guest of the African National University, which had been founded earlier in the century as the outcome of a spirit of intelligent cooperation on the part of the thinkers of the Ethiopian race both in the Mother Country and in their exiled home across the Atlantic.* Gradually it had come to dawn upon educationists that the error of blindly imitating Western methods must give place to original lines of racial intellectual development; and for that reason centers of learning were eager for information as to where mistakes had been made in the past, and how they might be remedied in the future.

Hampton has been described as one of the finest seats of learning in America. It is the work of Samuel Chapman Armstrong, a name which will ever be remembered with honor and veneration among cultured Ethiopians throughout the world, for it was left to him to point the way of freeing the souls of Africans in America after Abraham Lincoln and his stalwart men of iron will had freed their bodies.

It was "Emancipation Day," and the contrast between how the day was observed in earlier times on the plantations and the way the event was marked at Hampton on the occasion of Kwamankra's visit was extremely

* Hampton University is a historically black college in Hampton, Virginia, founded in 1868 by the American Missionary Association for the education of freed slaves. Its most famous alumnus in Casely Hayford's lifetime was Booker T. Washington.

remarkable. The boisterous, rowdy, senseless jubilation of young and old had given way to a purposeful intent to mark each passing year with some record of national progress and efficiency; and it was inspiring to see the modest manner and the dignified calm of the students as they filed into the Chapel Theater to the music of the University orchestra. But they had not long been seated when a low murmur could be heard all over the building which soon rose to a ringing cheer, as a side door opened, and the Principal of Hampton mounted the rostrum with Kwamankra and the professors following. Kwamankra had been announced to speak upon the work of Edward Wilmot Blyden, about the foremost thinker of the race, and great was the enthusiasm of the audience as with craned necks they took in every word of the speaker, as if it were a message from a new sphere.* The speaker dwelt on the broader outlook which Dr. Blyden had, for at least forty years, presented to his countrymen in his writings which he passed under review, dwelling upon each distinctive note, and wound up in the following graphic words:—

"The claim of Edward Wilmot Blyden to the esteem and regard of all thinking Africans rests not so much upon the special work he has done for any particular people of the African race, as upon the general work he has done for the race as a whole.

"The work of men like Booker T. Washington and W. E. Burghart Du Bois is exclusive and provincial. The work of Edward Wilmot Blyden is universal, covering the entire race and the entire race problem.

* As discussed in the introduction, Blyden was among the foremost influences on Casely Hayford and on nineteenth-century West African thought broadly. He is important here in particular because of his views on what he called Ethiopianism, which encouraged African Americans to return to the African continent to find redemption by contributing to its development. One of his major works, *African Life and Customs: Reprinted from "The Sierra Leone Weekly News"* (London: C. M. Phillips, 1908), is listed in "Suggested Further Reading" in this volume, as is Harry Nii Koney Odamtten's recent biography of Blyden's life and thoughts, *Edward W. Blyden's Intellectual Transformations: Afropublicanism, Pan-Africanism, Islam, and the Indigenous West African Church* (East Lansing: Michigan State University Press, 2019).

"What do I mean? I mean this: that while Booker T. Washington seeks to promote the material advancement of the black man in the United States, and W. E. Burghart Du Bois his social enfranchisement amid surroundings and in all atmosphere uncongenial to racial development, Edward Wilmot Blyden has sought for more than a quarter of a century to reveal everywhere the African unto himself; to fix his attention upon original ideas and conceptions as to his place in the economy of the world; to point out to him his work as a race among the races of men; lastly, and most important of all, to lead him back unto self-respect. He has been the voice of one crying in the wilderness all these years, calling upon all thinking Africans to go back to the rock whence they were hewn by the common Father of the nations—to drop metaphor, to learn to unlearn all that foreign sophistry has encrusted upon the intelligence of the African. Born in the West Indies some seventy years ago and nurtured in foreign culture, he has yet remained an African; and today he is the greatest living exponent of the true spirit of African nationality and manhood.

"To emphasize an important consideration, in the Afro-American school of thought the black man is seeking intellectually and materially to show himself a man along the lines of progress of the white man. In the African school of thought, represented by Dr. Blyden, the black man is engaged upon a sublimer task, namely, the discovery of his true place in creation upon natural and national lines. That is the striking difference between the two great schools of the thinkers of the race. And it has been the work of Edward Wilmot Blyden to accentuate this difference, and today he, of whom we are all so proud, is the leading thinker of the latter school of thought.*

"Apart from the magnetism of his personality, the great influence of Dr. Blyden over the rising thinking youth of the race, lies in the fact that he has revealed in his writings and utterances the true motive power which shall

* The school of thought referenced here is that of the "African personality," which posited a cultural and historical, rather than scientific, basis for separate lines of racial development. Blyden developed his views on Africans' distinctiveness in response to those of the overtly racist Anthropological Society of London, many of whose members considered African-descended people to be intrinsically inferior to Europeans.

carry the race on from victory unto victory. And all he has to say to his people, summing up his teaching in one word, is: man, know thyself.

"The voice that was aforetime crying solitarily in the wilderness has suddenly become the voice of a nation and of a people, calling unto their kindred across the Atlantic to come back to their way of thinking. We notice with a pang the strivings after the wind in which our brethren in America are engaged, and we ask them today to return to first principles and to original and racial conceptions—to those cooling streams by the fountains of Africa which would refresh their souls.

"To leave no possible doubt as to my meaning, Afro-Americans must bring themselves into touch with some of the general traditions and institutions of their ancestors, and, though sojourning in a strange land, endeavor to conserve the characteristics of the race. Thus and only thus, like Israel of old, will they be able, metaphorically, to walk out of Egypt in the near future with a great and a real spoil.

"Edward Wilmot Blyden is a leader among leaders of African aboriginal thought; and, lest a prophet should be without honor among his own kindred, I am happy on this occasion also to have, among others, the privilege and the opportunity of giving him the recognition that is his due."

For days and days the students of Hampton talked of little else besides the new conception of national aims presented in the address; and, in after years, it was noted that it gave a new color and meaning to the good racial work done at Hampton.

CHAPTER XVII

Race Emancipation—Particular Considerations: African Nationality

In the name of African nationality the thinker would, through the medium of *Ethiopia Unbound*, greet members of the race everywhere throughout the world. Whether in the east, south, or west of the African Continent, or yet among the teeming millions of Ethiopia's sons in America, the cry of the African, in its last analysis, is for scope and freedom in the struggle for existence, and it would seem as if the care of the leaders of the race has been to discover those avenues of right and natural endeavor which would, in the end, ensure for the race due recognition of its individuality.

The race problem is probably most intense in the United States of America, but there are indications that on the African Continent itself it is fast assuming concrete form. Sir Arthur Lawley, the present Governor of Madras, before leaving the Governorship of the Transvaal, is reported in a public address to have said that the "black peril" is a reality, and to have advised the whites to consolidate their forces in presence of the potential foe. The leaders of the race have hitherto exercised sound discretion and shown considerable wisdom in advising the African to follow the line of least resistance in meeting any combination of forces against him. The African's way to proper recognition lies not at present so much in the exhibition of material force and power, as in the gentler art of persuasion by the logic of facts and of achievements before which all reasonable men must bow.

A twofold danger threatens the African everywhere. It is the outcome of certain economic conditions whose method is the exploitation of the

Ethiopian for all he is worth. He is said to be pressed into the service of man, in reality, the service of the Caucasian. That being so, he never reaps the full meed of his work as a *man*. He materially contributes to the building of pavements on which he may not walk—take it as a metaphor, or as a fact, which way you please. He helps to work up revenues and to fill up exchequers over which, in most cases, he has no effective control, if any at all. In brief, he is labeled as belonging to a class apart among the races, and any attempt to rise above his station is terribly resented by the aristocracy of the races. Indeed, he is reminded at every turn that he is only intended to be a hewer of wood and a drawer of water. And so it happens that those among the favored sons of men who occasionally consider the lot of the Ethiopian are met with jeers and taunts. Is it any wonder, then, that even in the twentieth century, the African finds it terribly difficult to make headway even in his own country? The African may turn socialist, may preach and cry for reform until the day of judgment; but the experience of mankind shows this, that reform never comes to a class or a people unless and until those concerned have worked out their own salvation. And the lesson we have yet to learn is that we cannot depart from Nature's way and hope for real success.

And yet, it would seem as if in some notable instances the black man is bent upon following the line of greatest resistance in coping with the difficulties before him. Knowledge is the common property of mankind, and the philosophy which seeks for the Ethiopian the highest culture and efficiency in industrial and technical training is a sound one. It is well to arrest in favor of the race public opinion as to its capability in this direction. But that is not all, since there are certain distinctive qualities of race, of country, and of peoples which cannot be ignored without detriment to the particular race, country, or people. Knowledge, deprived of the assimilating element which makes it natural to the one taught, renders that person but a bare imitator. The Japanese, adopting and assimilating Western culture, of necessity commands the respect of Western nations, because there is something distinctly Eastern about him. He commands, to begin with, the uses of his native tongue, and has a literature of his own, enriched by translations from standard authors of other lands. He respects the institutions and customs of his ancestors, and there is an intelligent past which inspires him. He does not discard his national costume, and if, now and again, he dons Western attire, he does so as a matter of convenience, much as the Scotch, across the border, puts away, when the occasion demands it, his Highland costume. It is not the fault of the black man in America, for example, that he suffers today from the effects of a wrong that was inflicted upon him years ago by the forefathers of the very ones who now despise him. But he can see to it that as the years go by it becomes a matter of necessity for the American whites to respect and admire his manhood; and the surest way to the one or the other lies not so much in imitation as in originality and natural initiative. Not only must the Ethiopian acquire proficiency in the arts and sciences, in technical and industrial training, but he must pursue a course of scientific enquiry which would reveal to him the good things of the treasure house of his own nationality.

There are probably but a few men of African descent in America who, if they took the trouble by dipping into family tradition, would not be able to trace their connection and relationship with one or other of the great tribes of West Africa; and now that careful enquiry has shown that the institutions of the Aborigines of Africa are capable of scientific handling, what would be easier than for the great centers of culture and learning in the hands of Africans in the United States to found professorships in this relation? In the order of Providence, some of our brethren aforetime were suffered to be enslaved in America for a wise purpose. That event in the history of the race has made it possible for the speedier dissemination and adoption of the better part of Western culture; and today Africa's sons in the East and in the West can do peculiar service unto one another in the common cause of uplifting Ethiopia and placing her upon her feet among the nations. The East, for example, can take lessons from the West in the adoption of a sound educational policy, the kind of industrial and technical training which would enable aboriginals to make the best use of their lands and natural resources. And, surely, the West ought not to be averse to taking hints from the East as regards the preservation of national institutions, and the adoption of distinctive garbs and names, much as obtains among our friends the Japanese. While a student in London, a thrill of Oriental pride used to run through the writer when he brushed against an Asiatic in a garb distinctively Eastern. They aped no one. They were content to remain Eastern. For even when climatic conditions necessitated the adoption of European habiliments, they had sense enough to preserve some symbol of nationality. On the contrary, Africans would seem never to be content unless and until they make it possible for the European to write of them thus:

"How extraordinary is the spectacle of this huge race—millions of men—without land or language of their own, without traditions of the country they came from, bearing the very names of the men that enslaved them! . . .

"The black element is one which cannot be 'boiled down' into the great cosmopolitan American nation—the black man must always be tragically apart from the white man"*—and so on and so forth.

Now, if there is aught in the foregoing which is true to life, it bears but one meaning, namely, this, that the average Afro-American citizen of the United States has lost absolute touch with the past of his race, and is helplessly and hopelessly groping in the dark for affinities that are not natural, and for effects for which there are neither national nor natural causes. That being so, the African in America is in a worse plight than the Hebrew in Egypt. The one preserved his language, his manners and customs, his religion and household gods; the other has committed national suicide, and at present it seems as if the dry bones of the vision have no life in them. Looking at the matter closely, it is not so much *Afro-Americans* that we want as *Africans* or *Ethiopians*, sojourning in a strange land, who, out of a full heart and a full knowledge can say: If I forget thee, Ethiopia, let my right hand forget its cunning! Let us look at the other side of the picture. How extraordinary would be the spectacle of this huge Ethiopian race—some millions of men—having imbibed all that is best in Western culture in the land of their oppressors, yet remaining true to racial instincts and inspiration, customs

* This quote appeared originally in 1905 in London's *National Review* newspaper (volume 45), which was founded in 1883 as an outlet for the British Conservative Party.

and institutions, much as did the Israelites of old in captivity! When this more pleasant picture will have become possible of realization, then, and only then, will it be possible for our people in bondage "metaphorically to walk out of Egypt in the near future with a great and a real spoil."

Someone may say, but, surely, you don't mean to suggest that questions of dress and habits of life matter in the least. I reply emphatically, they do. They go to the root of the Ethiopian's self-respect. Without servile imitation of our teachers in their get-up and manner of life, it stands to reason that the average white man would regard the average black man far more seriously than he does at present. The adoption of a distinctive dress for the cultured African, therefore, would be a distinct step forward, and a gain to the cause of Ethiopian progress and advancement. Pray listen to the greatest authority on national life upon this matter, "Behold, I have taught you statutes and judgments even as the Lord God commanded me that ye should do in the land whither ye go to possess it. Keep, therefore, and do them: for this is your wisdom and your understanding in the sight of the nations which shall hear these statutes and say, surely, this great nation is a wise and understanding people." Yes, my people are pursuing knowledge as for a hidden treasure, and have neglected wisdom and true understanding, and hence are they daily a laughing stock in the sight of the nations.

Here, then, is work for cultured West Africans to start a reform which will be worldwide in its effects among Ethiopians, remembering as a basis that we, as a people, have our own statutes, the customs and institutions of our forefathers, which we cannot neglect and live. We on the Gold Coast are making a huge effort in this direction, and though European habits will die hard with some of our people, the effort is worth making; and, if we don't succeed quite with this generation, we shall succeed with the next. That the movement is gaining ground may well be gathered from the following extract from the *Gold Coast Leader* of 24th February, 1907, reporting the coronation of Ababio IV, *Mantse*, that is King, of "British Accra." Says the correspondent: "For the first time I realized that the Gold Coast would be more exhilarating and enjoyable indeed if the educated inhabitants in it would hark back to the times of old and take a few lessons in the art and grace of the sartorial simplicity and elegance of their forebears. The 'scholars' looked quite noble and full of dignity in the native dress. There was not one ignoble or mean person among them, and so for the matter of that did the ladies."

Then I should like to see *Ethiopian Leagues* formed throughout the United States much in the same way as the *Gaelic League* in Ireland for the purpose of studying and employing Fante, Yoruba, Hausa, or other standard African language, in daily use. The idea may seem extraordinary on the first view, but if you are inclined to regard it thus, I can only point to the examples of Ireland and Denmark, who have found the vehicle of a national language much the safest and most natural way of national conservancy and evolution. If the Dane and Irish find it expedient in Europe, surely the matter is worthy of consideration by the Ethiopian in the United States, in Sierra Leone, in the West Indies, and in Liberia.

A distinguished writer, dwelling upon the advantages of culture in a people's own language, said: "These are important considerations of a highly practical kind. Ten years ago, we had in Ireland a people divorced, by half a century of education conducted along alien lines, from their own proper language and culture. We had also in Ireland a people seemingly incapable of rational action, sunk in hopeless poverty, apparently doomed to disappear. We have in Ireland today the beginnings of a system of education in the national language and along national lines; and we have at the same time, and in the places where this kind of education has been operative, an unmistakable advance in intellectual capacity and material prosperity." Now, if the soul that is in the Ethiopian, even in the United States, remains Ethiopian, which it does, to judge from the coon songs which have enriched the sentiment of mankind by their pathos, then, I say, the foregoing words, true as everyone must admit they are, point distinctly to the impossibility of departing from *nature's* way with any hope of lasting good to African nationality. I do sincerely trust these thoughts will catch the eye of such distinguished educationists as Mr. Booker T. Washington and others of the United States and in the West Indies as also the attention of similar workers in West Africa who have the materials ready at hand. It is a great work, but I do believe that my countrymen have the heart and the intelligence to grapple with it successfully.

CHAPTER XVIII

Race Emancipation: The Crux of the Matter

One of the most pathetic passages in the history of human thought is the remarkable work of an Ethiopian, "The Souls of Black Folk," written by the well-known thinker, W. P. B. Du Bois, of Atlanta, Ga., in the United States of America. It deals with a matter which has attracted the attention of all thinking men of modern times. European writers have dealt with the question, and so have African and American writers. But the particular standpoint of Mr. Du Bois is peculiar unto itself. It recalls the story of the Hebrew people; but neither at the stage of actual enslavement, nor yet at the hour of emancipation. As yet, the people are roaming aimlessly in the wilderness, and the leaders, though having the promise, have but a glimmer of light to see distantly a day of deliverance possible. It is true twenty, thirty, years of the forty are past, and the full light may break some day all of a sudden; but even now the mighty arms of Moses must be upraised and supported lest the chosen people perish by the way.*

It has been said that Mr. Du Bois' attitude toward the race question is a pathetic one. "I am a problem," our author would seem to say. Then presently

* Hebrew tradition recounts a fight between the Israelites, the chosen of God, and the Amalekites. Moses stood at the top of a hill with the staff of God in his hands. For as long as he held up his hands, the Israelites were winning; when he lowered them, their enemies would take the lead. To ensure their victory, two of his companions held up his hands until sunset, and the Israelites won the battle (Exodus 17:8–16). The author is making a clear comparison between Black people and the Israelites, who spent a significant portion of their history in captivity or fighting for the preservation and protection of their heritage.

follows the plaintive query: "How does it feel to be a problem?" To descend to particulars, he says: "After the Egyptian and Indian, the Greek and Roman, the Teuton and Mongolian, the Negro is a sort of seventh son, born with a veil, and gifted with second sight in this American world—a world which yields him no true self-consciousness, but only lets him see himself through the revelation of the other world. It is a peculiar sensation, this double consciousness, this sense of always looking at one's self through the eyes of others, of measuring one's soul by the tape of a world that looks on in amused contempt and pity. One ever feels his twoness—an American, a Negro; two souls, two thoughts, two unreconciled strivings; two warring ideals in one dark body, whose dogged strength alone keeps it from being torn asunder." Ah! there's the rub! Poor Ethiopia! how sorely hath the iron of oppression entered into the very soul of thy erring children!

Now, self-consciousness obviously depends upon self-revelation after which comes self-realization. But has the Ethiopian sojourning in America, and, for that matter, even in Liberia and in Sierra Leone ever realized himself? Has he received that self-awakening which would move him, in the words of the prodigal, to exclaim, "Alas me! How many hired servants of my father's have bread enough and to spare and I perish with hunger?" No, it has not yet occurred to him to arise and go to his Father, regardless of the taunts of the surly elder son. He perceives not yet that the Father is waiting to make a feast of rejoicing over the emancipation of his soul. No, he will not yet don the robe of sonship, nor suffer the ring, the symbol of a spiritual union and equality, to be placed upon his finger. Poor man! Instead of the fatted calf, he still sits sulkily by the wayside over Jordan apples which presently turn into ashes in his mouth. Listen to his cry: "Who shall deliver me from the burden of these unreconciled and irreconcilable strivings?" Listen! Not so long as he turns away from the Father's house and elects to remain a slave in soul. To be a puzzle unto others is not to be a puzzle unto one's self. The sphinx in the Temple of the Sphinx in ancient Egypt is a recumbent figure with the head of a lion, but with the features of King Chephron, the Master of Egypt, somewhere about 3960 B.C. Now, fancy Candace, Queen of Ethiopia, or Chephron, the Master of Egypt, being troubled with a double consciousness. Watch that symbolic, reposeful figure yonder, and you can but see one soul, one ideal, one striving, one line of a natural, rational progress. Look again, and you must agree that the idea of a double consciousness is absurd with these representative types. It is true that—

> "Bowed by the weight of centuries, he leans
> Upon his hoe and gazes on the ground;
> The emptiness of ages in his face,
> And on his back the burden of the world."*

But, surely, to bear the burden of others, one should have thought, is honorable work, and the toiling one need not be a problem unto himself.

It is apparent that Mr. Du Bois writes from an American standpoint, surrounded by an American atmosphere. And, of course, it is not his fault, for he knows of no other. To be born an African in America, in that great commonwealth of dollars and the merciless aggrandizement of the individual, where the weak must look out for himself, and the cry of the innocent appeals not to him who rides triumphantly to fortune, is to be entangled in conditions which give no room for the assertion of the highest manhood. African manhood demands that the Ethiopian should seek not his opportunity, or ask for elbow room, from the white man, but that he should create the one or the other for himself.

Thoughts like these were stirring men's minds when the Pan-African Conference met in the Gold Coast in the year 1905, at the invitation of the Gold Coast Aborigines Rights Protection Society, that prototype of the kind of African National Assemblies which must be called into being in the near

* These lines are from an 1899 poem called "The Man with the Hoe" by the American poet Edwin Markham, which in turn was inspired by the French landscape painter Jean-François Millet's 1862 painting by the same name. The poem was hugely popular and widely translated, bringing international attention to the cause of labor reform in its grandiose description of a toiling peasant.

future for the solution of African questions.* Among the distinguished speakers at the Conference was Kwamankra, and great was the impression which was created by the paper which he read upon Dr. Blyden's great work upon "African Life and Customs," which is here recorded. Said he:

"I have followed, with keen interest, the series of articles on 'African Life and Customs' in the *Sierra Leone Weekly News* from the ever instructive pen of Dr. Blyden; and, perhaps, the following thoughts, suggested by them, may be useful to the student of African problems, seeking for the conditions suitable for Race Emancipation.

"I believe it was the learned doctor who first pointed out that Africa needs no redemption. But that she requires emancipation from the thralldom of foreign ideas inimical to racial development, few will doubt. What, indeed, can be more certain than that the African in the United States, in the West Indies, and in the mother country, East, West and South, has need to unlearn a good deal? But the unfortunate part of it is that the way out is at yet but dimly dawning even upon such as would otherwise be qualified to lead the masses. It becomes, therefore, the sacred duty of those who can see a little more clearly ahead to point the way. Hence it is that, in season and out of season, the warning voice of our grand old man is heard.

"The African who comes to his brethren with a red-hot civilization straight from Regent Circus, or the Boulevards of Paris, and cries anathema to all black folk who would not adopt his views or mode of life, is, perhaps, not the man who is, or can be, of much help in developing African life and African idiosyncrasies along the line of natural and healthy development. That is,

* The first Pan-African Conference was held in London in July of 1900, and was attended by thirty-seven delegates mainly from the United States and the West Indies, including W. E. B. Du Bois. The three-day meeting was organized mainly by the Trinidadian barrister Henry Sylvester Williams, and an attorney named A. F. Ribeiro represented the Gold Coast. Williams established the Pan-African Association in the wake of the event and intended for it to gather every two years. Though that plan ultimately failed, the conference paved the way for the smaller 1905 Gold Coast meeting, and eventually, for a more famous series of eight Pan-African Congresses between 1919 and 2014.

perhaps, the underlying teaching, if not the sum total of the teaching, of the series of articles now before us.

"Africa seems destined for ever to be a land of mystery. When, in our modern way, we have demolished African strongholds, and, with the wantonness of an iconoclast, saved nothing to remind us of the artistic past and future possibilities of the people—nay, when we have laid out streets and encouraged shops to spring up mushroom-like here and there, we think we have solved the mystery of the gods, while, all the time, the heart of the matter is not reached. In many a forest glen they dwell in their tens and in their hundreds, but seldom in their thousands, undisturbed by the vulgar eye. Your cities are not their cities, your tinsel is not their gold. All they ask for is for as little interference as possible. What can you do with such a people, except to give them scope and room for natural development?

"I am writing this on the verandah of a house in the main street of Kumasi. Where once stood the palace of the King, now stands an ugly coast building with dirty blinds and a dirtier shop below. But the men and the women are not changed. The type is pronounced; and as I watch them passing up and down in different groups, it is easy to see that the men and women, who walked the banks of the Nile in days of yore, are not far different from the remnants of the sons of *Efua Kobi*. As you see the new unfinished coast houses side by side of the frail impermanent, quadrangular compounds of the old type, the thought suggests itself to you that, after all, it is the intangible that matters. You see you enter one of these compounds, and you find but bare, open rooms, in the case of a Chief's house, often supported by pillars. Where do these people actually live? Where do they keep their treasures, and their household gods? No one can tell you. But they are as safe as the golden stool itself is.* Thus you

* Akan kings traditionally sit on special stools carved from wood. The golden stool symbolizes the divine power and the very soul of the Asante nation. It is believed to have been conjured from the sky for the first Asante king by Ɔkɔmfo Anokye, a legendary High Priest of great power and accomplishments. Given its importance to their history and identity, the Asante have gone to war over the golden stool, notably when a British governor of the Gold Coast demanded that it be handed over so he could sit on it.

arrive at the heart of these people, and you are inwardly persuaded that all the symbols of European authority, responsibility, and opportunity are more impermanent than the frail houses you see about you. How to reach the heart of such a people would not be an uninteresting study. If you succeed, you have arrived at the heart of the principle which may be safely applied to healthy race development wheresoever necessary.

"Once more, then, Ashanti is my type, for the reason that Ashanti is yet unspoiled by the bad methods of the missionary.

"I remember once seeing Rev. Ramsay in Kumasi. He told me he had labored in Ashanti off and on for forty years. I asked how many Ashantis he had in his church at Kumasi proper? He said, thirty. His assistant corrected him and said fifty. I asked him how many in all Ashanti? About two hundred. Not quite so many, his assistant concurring. Rev. Asare, the assistant, and his good wife are both Africans, who have adopted the European habit. I had visited the missionaries in my African costume. They agreed, including my African friends, that it was appropriate. I hope the object lesson was not without significance to the hopes of the success of their mission. But, however that may be, today the Ashanti goes unconcerned of the white man's religion and of the white man's ways, as ancient Egypt might have done.

"What is religion? If it is that which links back the finite to the infinite, the material to the spiritual, the temporal to the eternal—that which inspires an unfaltering faith in a life beyond the grave, then, I maintain, that the African, in his system of philosophy, gives place to none.

"Hark! What are those suggestive words I catch from the so-called Fetish chant that the priest, called to attend a dying man, is humming in a low, doleful voice!

'Midan, Nyami, Kwiaduampon,
Midan, Nyami, Kwiadu,
Nyame ama, Nyami ama
Nyami na wama mi akom!'

Meaning:

> 'On God I depend, the impregnable Rock;
> On God I depend, the impregnable Rock.
> God has given, God has given,
> God has given me the priesthood.'

I have loosely rendered the word '*Kwiaduampon*' as 'the impregnable rock,' but etymologically, it conveys the idea of 'the ever faithful God.'

"Now, when, in the face of all this you tell the so-called pagan that he will not end well, that he is the devil's own, he listens curiously, and wonders whether you can mean all you say. His attitude henceforth is a defensive one, seldom antagonistic. Henceforth he only asks to be let alone. And yet people wonder that so-called spiritual work makes such little headway in these parts. And the land had rest forty years. Do you not see the purport of it all? It has not pleased the gods to disturb her. Leave her in peace, the slumbering sphinx, until the God of Ethiopia wakes her up! For it is not so much religion that she wants as knowledge—knowledge that will enable her to explain to the waiting world the faith that is in her and the reason of her being.

"According to Dr. Freeman, in his History of Europe, the word pagan originally meant a countryman, and, by extension, a worshipper of false gods. Well, Paul, before the application of the phrase, spoke of a temple with the inscription 'to the unknown God,' whom men ignorantly worshipped. Evident, therefore, it is that a pagan is not necessarily a worshipper of false gods. Even Marcus Aurelius persecuted the Christians; yet it is conceivable that had he lived in a later age, he would have set his philosophical sayings in terms of Christianity.

"If Christ and God are one, those who worship God ignorantly, worship Christ ignorantly, and it were better for the many to worship in spirit and in truth that which they know fully, but as it were through a glass darkly, rather than don the intellectual garb which ends in questioning the Divinity of Christ, and by parity of reasoning, according to the theologians, the Divinity of God.

"In the philosophy of the West African there is no reason why Christ should not be God. For to him man is half God and half man. But a thin veil divides the finite from the infinite, and when Death pulls aside the curtain, there is no knowing what one shall be. Indeed, it is conceivable that paganism, scientifically interpreted, may place the Christ on a higher pedestal than Christianity has yet done. What the unspoiled educated African feels he wants is, rest—rest to think out his own thoughts, and to work out his own salvation.

"Have we, who advocate these views, lost faith in Christianity? It does not follow. It was Dr. Blyden who wrote in the 'Significance of Liberia' these remarkable words: . . . 'I am sure that Christianity, as conceived and modified in Europe and America, with its oppressive hierarchy, its caste prejudices and limitations, its pecuniary burdens and exactions, its injurious intermeddling in the harmless and useful customs of alien peoples, is not the Christianity of Christ. But I am sure, also, that the Christianity of Christ is no cunningly devised fable, no *ignis fatuus*, to disappear in darkness and confusion. I am sure that its spirit will ultimately prevail in the proceedings of men; that the knowledge of the Lord shall cover the earth as the waters cover the sea. I am sure that Jesus, upon whom is the spirit of the Lord, because He hath anointed Him to preach the gospel to the poor, to heal the broken-hearted, to preach deliverance to the captive, the recovery of sight to the blind, to set at liberty them that are bruised; I am sure that this

> "Jesus shall reign where'er the sun
> Doth his successive journeys run!"*

I am sure, also, that all counterfeits, however bright or real they look, must vanish as the truth appears. We should not be discouraged because the system bearing the name of Christ makes no progress on this Continent—that it lingers, halts, and limps on the threshold of the great opportunity. Jesus is

* A hymn written by Isaac Watts (1674–1748), a British minister. "Jesus Shall Reign" is one of his most well-known hymns and is said to be inspired by psalm 72.

lame. He has been wounded in the house of his friends. We must bind up his wounds. Treading in the footsteps of our immortal countryman, we must bear the Cross after Jesus. We must strip him of the useless, distorting, and obstructive habiliments by which he has been invested by the materializing sons of Japhet.* Let Him be lifted up as he really is, that He may be seen, pure and simple, by the African, and He will draw all men unto Him!'

"The broader outlook upon religion is the lot of the careless Ethiopian. He need not necessarily see God except through Christ, but is, withal, so Catholic that he can speak of the universal

'Strife that won our life
With the incarnate Son of God.'

"A significant marriage took place in Sierra Leone in March of the present year. A highly cultured African gentleman was married to a Mohammedan lady. Of this lady the *Weekly News* of 21st March, 1908, says: 'There has been no attempt to unmake her, no inducement to make her alter the religion of her fathers or her native dress.' I remember overhearing an argument in a railway carriage between two educated Africans as to the effect of such marriages. They were both Sierra Leone men; and the sore point with one of the controversialists was as to how her ladyship would be received at Government House, or how she would receive at home the friends of her lord and master. Here you have the two warring elements in national development: 'What is it that the white man expects me to do? What is it that I am called upon in reason and by nature to do?' Between these two the manhood of the race is throttled and sacrificed on the altar of convenience.

* Japheth is one of the three sons of Noah in the Bible. Ham, his brother, was cursed by Noah after an incident involving Noah's nakedness. Centuries later, the curse of Ham was used to justify the enslavement of Black people, considered to be Ham's descendants. In that narrative, Japheth is considered to be the father of Europeans. This is in spite of the fact that the Bible does not accord importance to skin color in the incident among Noah and his sons.

"Now, what appears remarkable in Sierra Leone would not be remarkable on the Gold Coast, where it is common for educated men to mate with less privileged women. And the reason, founded on common sense, is not far to seek. Between the African woman who, collecting firewood in a plantation, overpowered by nature, brings her little one into the world, soothes it, and carries it safely home with her load and the African lady who talks of going *home*, meaning Europe, to be confined, there is a mighty difference. The latter is the product of an effete system of training, and it and the system will perish out of hand. The former has a foundation in character that will bear the weight of the ages as far as African life and work are concerned.

"With respect to marriage a great blunder has been committed by the meddlesome missionaries, namely, 'that of forcing a life of hypocrisy upon those whom they compass earth and sea to get into the fold. Whereas the average so-called convert was, before he came into the church, living a fairly decent, open, life in his marital relations, embracing Christianity invariably meant for him adopting subterfuges and chicanery to cover up the way of the old life, which not all the spiritual graces could help him to brush aside.'

"There is a vulgar way of approaching the question of polygamy; there is the scientific way; and lastly there is the spiritual way. It may appear strange to the average man that there is a spiritual side to polygamy. Yet on second thought it must be so. In this, as in other matters, evil be to him who evil thinks.

"The crux of the educational question, as it affects the African, is that Western methods denationalize him. He becomes a slave to foreign ways of life and thought. He will desire to be a slave no longer. So far is this true that the moment the unspoiled educated African shows initiative and asserts an individuality, his foreign mentor is irritated by the phenomenon. In September, 1905, public events on the Gold Coast led me to write in the local press as follows: 'We feel, secondly, that the educated native is unduly maligned for party purposes. It is the same cry as the educated Welsh, Irish, or Scotch. In any case, it is a childish cry—a sign of weakness. Does a native cease to be a native when once he is educated?. . . . But for the educated native, where would the unsophisticated native be? Hence the weakness of the cry—the shibboleth of the 'educated native.' Heaven grant that the educated native may never be wanting in his duty to his less privileged brethren, or betray their trust in him.'

"But let there be no mistake about the matter. The foregoing strictly applies to the unspoiled cultured African. The other type is no good to anybody. The superfine African gentleman, who, at the end of every second or third year, talks of a run to Europe, lest there should be a nervous breakdown, may be serious or not, but is bound in time to be refined off the face of the African continent.

"And now I come to the question of questions: 'How may the West African be trained so as to preserve his national identity and race instincts?'

"As a precautionary measure, I would take care to place the educational seminary in a region far beyond the reach of the influence of the coast. If I were founding a national University for the Gold Coast and for Ashanti, I would make a suitable suburb of Kumasi the center. But why do I speak of a national University? For the simple reason that you cannot educate a people unless you have a suitable training ground. A Tuskegee Institute is very useful in its way, but where would you get the teachers unless you drew them from the ranks of the University trained men? And since even the teachers must be first locally trained, the highest training ground becomes a necessity.

"I would found in such a University a Chair for History; and the kind of history that I would teach would be universal history with particular reference to the part Ethiopia has played in the affairs of the world. I would lay stress upon the fact that while Rameses II was dedicating temples to 'the God of gods and secondly to his own glory,' the God of the Hebrews had not yet appeared unto Moses in the burning bush; that Africa was the cradle of the world's systems and philosophies, and the nursing mother of its religions. In short, that Africa has nothing to be ashamed of of its place among the nations of the earth. I would make it possible for this seat of learning to be the means of revising erroneous current ideas regarding the African; of raising him in self-respect; and of making him an efficient co-worker in the uplifting of man to nobler effort.

"Then I should like to see professorships for the study of the Fante, Hausa, and Yoruba languages. The idea may seem odd upon the first view. But if you are inclined to regard it thus, I can only point to the examples of Ireland and Denmark, who have found the vehicle of a national language much the safest and most natural way of national conservancy and evolution. If the Dane and Irish find it expedient in Europe, surely the matter is worthy of consideration by the African. Says Mr. James O'Hannay, writing on the work of the Irish League and the influence of a national language in the November, 1905, number of the *Independent Review*, at pages 311 and 312: 'Our history, our customs, our characters are unintelligible to us until we know it. Character, for instance, is the result of inheritance and environment; and there is no more subtly influential environment than the language we speak. If these two are in opposition, if a people inherits a Celtic spirit and grows up in an Anglo-Saxon atmosphere, with the English language on its lips, what kind of character will result? It is likely that a people tossed in this cross sideway of contradictions will tend to develop inconsistencies of character—amazing force rendered useless by recurring spasms of weakness, brilliant intellectual capacity sterilized by inability to grasp the conditions of material progress, and so forth.'

"If you want a further support to this view, you have it laid down in an interview with Mr. A. G. Fraser (Trinity College, Oxford), the Principal of Trinity College, Kandy, Ceylon. Says the *Times* reporter: 'He laid special stress on the importance of conducting the training given in Indian Colleges on a vernacular basis rather than through the medium of English, as is too often the case at present. The system existing in most missionary and Government schools tends distinctly to separate those thus educated from their own race. He advocated education almost on Japanese lines, *i.e.*, thorough teaching of English as a subject and literature, but the teaching of science, engineering, medicine, etc., through the medium of the vernacular, and not of English—with a complete connection between the village school and the central college.'

"Moreover, I would make this seat of learning so renowned and attractive that students from the United States, the West Indies, Sierra Leone, and Liberia, as well as from Lagos and the Gambia, would flock to it. And they would come to this Mecca—this *alma mater* of national conservancy, not in top hat and broad cloth, but in the sober garb in which the Romans conquered the material world, and in which we may conquer the spiritual world.

"Now, it is easy to see that the graduates that such a school will turn out will be *men*—no effete, mongrel, product of foreign systems.

"When three or four years back I had the pleasure of accompanying Dr. Blyden to the Royal Academy, he drew my particular attention to a famous picture, representing the wolf and the lamb as dwelling together, etc. After we had both drunk in the beauty of portraiture for a while, he gravely remarked: 'and a little child shall lead them—that is Africa.' I was struck by the allusion, and I still think there is a deal in the reflection. But it has since struck me also, that it is not the spoiled educated African that may be expected to help in the regenerative work of the world. The unspoiled son of the tropics, nursed in a tropical atmosphere, favorable to the growth of national life, he it is who may show us the way.

"The voice of the ancient universal God goes forth once more, who will go for us, who will show us any good? May there be a full, free, and hearty response from the sons of Ethiopia in the four quarters of the globe."

CHAPTER XIX

A Similitude: The Greek and the Fante

By this time the precocious youth was well on in his teens, and was already grappling with the intricacies of Greek roots and Latin suffixes. But often would his father warn him to be mindful more of the things which matter, as he quaintly put it. Now and again he would induce the youth to draw comparisons between the mode of thought and the practice of the ancients; and he would insist that there was no better intellectual, moral, and national training for a young Fante than such exercise involved. By way of encouragement, when the youth had done particularly well, he would take him upon new ground and delight him with stories from Homer's great masterpiece, which, in a curious way, reflected the everyday life of their own people.*

On this particular occasion, you may well imagine the excitement of Ekra Kwow, as he drew a low stool beside the paterfamilias, all eagerness for the latter to begin. The youth looked disappointed, as, instead of beginning a story, his father continued smoking, and simply thrust into his hand an old, well-thumbed popular edition of the story of the Odyssey, done into beautiful English by the Rev. Alfred J. Church.

* Casely Hayford is referring here to *The Odyssey*, which recounts Odysseus's journey home after the Trojan War. Between scenes of epic action are calmer moments where we read of Greek customs and practices, such as the ones that Kwamankra is about to discuss with his son. The links that Kwamankra makes between the African and Ancient Greek cultures echo a history of scholars who promote a more Afrocentric view of Antiquity. See Cheikh Anta Diop, *The African Origin of Civilization: Myth or Reality* (New York: Lawrence Hill Books, 1997) and Martin Bernal, *Black Athena: The Afroasiatic Roots of Classical Civilization* (New Brunswick: Rutgers University Press, 2020), included in the "Suggested Further Reading" list in this volume.

"What is the matter, father; are you not well tonight?"

"That's not it, my boy. I am as well as ever, thank you. But tonight I want you to read to me instead. I want to see how you handle Mr. Church's beautiful setting of the great thoughts of the master. You know to some this feast of the gods is like throwing pearls before swine. But go on. Begin with the visit of Athené to Nausicaa, the daughter of King Alcinoüs."

Thus the youth began: "Athené spake, saying, why hath thy mother so careless a child, Nausicaa? Lo! thy raiment lieth unwashed, and yet the day of thy marriage is at hand, when thou must have fine clothing for thyself, and to give to them that shall lead thee to thy bridegroom's house; for thus doth a bride win good repute. Do thou, therefore, arise with the day, and go to wash the raiment, and I will go with thee . . .

"And when the morning was come, Nausicaa awoke, marveling at the dream, and went seeking her parents. Her mother she found busy with her maidens at the loom, spinning yarn dyed with purple of the sea, and her father she met as he was going to the Council with the Chiefs of the land. Then she said: 'Give me, Father, the wagon with the mules that I may take the garments to the river to wash them'. . . .

"Then he called to the men, and they made ready the wagon, and harnessed the mules; and the maiden brought the raiment out of her chamber and put it in the wagon. Also her mother filled a basket with all manner of food, and poured wine in a goat-skin bottle. Olive oil also she gave her, that Nausicaa and her maidens might anoint themselves after the bath. And Nausicaa took the reins and touched the mules with the whip. Then was there a clatter of hoofs, and the mules went on with their load, nor did they grow weary."

As the youth stopped for a second to take breath, Kwamankra exclaimed, "That's good. Does that remind you of anything you see daily around you?"

The youth paused for a moment, and then said: "It looks very much like how the Fante women prepare to do their washing in the brook, and it is curious the mention of the use of oil to anoint the body after a bath. Why, that's just what our people do."

"Good; powers of observation fair, my boy," remarked Kwamankra proudly. "You see in these extra-civilized days the laundress and the charwoman do the cleansing of our soiled linen, and who would dream of seeing a king's daughter doing her own washing, let alone her father's, or her brother's. Yet, in ancient Greece it was not so. The highest in birth preserved native simplicity, much as the unspoiled among our own people do unto this day. Then there are just one or two points you have missed in the narrative. Alcinoüs is described as a king. His daughter meets him as he is going to the Council with the chiefs of the land. There is something strikingly in accord with our own custom here—just what an *Omanhin* would do."

"Lo! thy raiment lieth unwashed, and yet the day of thy marriage is at hand, when thou must have fair clothing for thyself, *and to give to them that shall lead thee to thy bridegroom's house*," he quoted, and then added, "thus do we in marriage and in death provide for the kinsmen and the kinswomen who lead us."

As the youth began to understand what the paterfamilias had meant by "the things which matter," he read with far greater expression the inimitable passages which describe the meeting of Ulysses with Nausicaa, her kindly address and hospitality, and his introduction to the Court of King Alcinoüs. And such a Court! "A wondrous place it was, with walls of brass and doors of gold, hanging on posts of silver; and on either side of the door were dogs of gold and silver, the work of Hephæstus and against the wall all along from the threshold to the inner chamber, were set seats, on which sat the chiefs of the Phæcians feasting; and youths wrought in gold stood holding torches in their hands, to give light in the darkness. Fifty women were in the house grinding corn and weaving robes, for the women of the land are no less skilled to weave than are the men to sail the sea. And round about the house were gardens beautiful exceedingly, with orchards of fig, and apple, and pear, and pomegranate, and olive. Drought hurts them not, nor frost, and harvest comes after harvest without ceasing. Also there was a vineyard; and some of the grapes were parching in the sun, and some were being gathered, and some again were but just turning red. And there were beds of all manner of flowers; and in the midst of all were two fountains which never failed."

"And yet," observed Kwamankra, "the daughter of King Alcinoüs was not above cleansing soiled linen; and there is something sweetly simple and familiar, as you see Ulysses bidden unto the feast, and an attendant pours water on his hands, and he is given meat and drink thereafter, and in all this the Fante-born feels himself particularly at home with these Grecians."

"Indeed," pursued Kwamankra, "as one turns over the wonderful pages of the story of the Odyssey, he stumbles across such similitudes of thought and action, as between the Greek and the Fante, that are simply amazing."

"Tell me all about that," snapped up the youth eagerly.

"Well," continued Kwamankra, "in no phase of Grecian thought is this more striking than in the conception of the Deity. The great *Niakrapon*, or *Nyami*, of the Fante corresponds with the *Zeus* of the Greek, as *Abusum* correspond with the lesser gods; and when the Greek speaks of the 'oracle of the god in the midst of an oak tree,' he conveys the same idea as the Fante does when he speaks of the *busum* in an *odoom* tree, popularly described as fetish. Again, similarly, when the Fante makes an invocation, it is upon *Nyiakrapon* he calls, '*Mika Nyiakrapon*,' as distinguished from any of the *Abusum*, or lesser gods, just in the same way as the Greek would say, 'Would to God,' as distinguished from any of the lesser gods. Moreover, the spiritual sense of the Greek was as keen as that of the Fante. The gods of the Fante mix today as freely with mortals as did Proteus, Poseidon, or Athené, the daughter of Zeus; and their offices are the same, for, if men paid heed, they would still gather inspiration for action as in the days when Athene came down from Olympus, and said unto doubting Ulysses, 'Verily, thou art weak in faith. Some put their trust in men, yet men are weaker than the gods; why trustest not thou in me? Verily, I am with thee, and will keep thee to the end. But now sleep, for to watch all the night is vexation of spirit.'"*

* In Akan religious belief, there is a Supreme Being who is also the Creator of all. Humans revere this God, in addition to Mother Earth, the ancestors, and what are sometimes termed

"Why," quoth the youth, "that reads like a passage in the Bible."

"Yes," the thinker went on musingly; "God hath not spoken to man only in the Hebrew Scriptures. But I was going to say, and so one might go on almost *ad infinitum*, gathering pearls of thought at every turn. Take, for instance, the incident when Penelope says to Eumæus, 'Call now this stranger; didst thou not mark how my son sneezed a blessing when I spake?' I do not know whether the idea of sneezing a blessing occurs in any other language; but a Fante says: '*Akam yey*' when you sneeze in his presence, exactly expressing the same idea. Again, the customs of offering sacrifice to the gods, and making libation to gods and deceased ancestors, are common alike to the two peoples. And when you recall the familiar way in which the poet speaks of Eurybates, the herald of Ulysses, 'Older than he, dark-skinned, round in the shoulders, with curly hair,' it dawns upon the Ethiopian that he gains vastly more in self-respect by intimate acquaintance with the ancient Greek than with the modern Saxon.

> Let nothing be done through strife or vain-glory; but in lowliness of mind let each esteem others better than themselves.
> Look not every man on his own things, but every man also on the things of others.
> Let this mind be in you, which was also in Christ Jesus:
> Who, being in the form of God, thought it not robbery to be equal with God:
> But made himself of no reputation,
> And took upon him the form of a servant,
> And was made in the likeness of men.
> And being found in fashion as a man, he humbled himself, and became obedient unto death, even the death of the Cross.

"lesser" or "smaller" gods (*abosom*). Even though "fetish" is tied to the belief that an object may have spiritual powers, the word also has derogatory connotations that come from the colonial encounter. There are, of course, similarities between the Akan pantheon and the Greek. There are also vast differences.

WHEREFORE

God also hath highly exalted him,
And given him a name
Which is above every name,
That at the name of Jesus
Every knee should bow;
Of things in heaven,
And things in earth,
And things under the earth;
And that every tongue should confess that Jesus Christ
is Lord, to the glory of God the Father.—Paul. *

The tumult and the shouting dies;
The Captains and the Kings depart:
Still stands thine ancient sacrifice,
A humble and a contrite heart.
Lord God of Hosts, be with us yet,
Lest we forget—lest we forget!—Kipling. †

---

* Paul's letter to the Philippians, 2:3–11.

† Rudyard Kipling (1865–1936) is one of Victorian England's most famous writers. He was born in Bombay to English parents and spent some of his childhood years in India. This extract is from his 1897 poem "Recessional." A recessional hymn is sung or played at the end of a church service, and Kipling wrote this poem to commemorate Queen Victoria's Diamond Jubilee. An imperialist poet, Kipling also wrote the infamous "The White Man's Burden" (1899) to encourage imperial conquest and to justify colonization as a moral obligation white people had to civilize others. Kipling won the Nobel Prize for Literature in 1907.

CHAPTER XX

And a Little Child Shall Lead Them

By the year 1925 a mighty change had come over the thought of the nations, and it was due to some extent to the work of the *Gold Coast Nation and Ethiopian Review*, promoted by Kwamankra just before the close of the first ten years of the century in the interests of Gold Coast national conservancy; but as time went on it had broadened out in sympathy to embrace the needs of the entire race. During the preceding fifteen years the *Nation* had freely circulated throughout the Ethiopian world, and the promoter and the Editors were in constant communication with the leading thinkers of the race throughout the world.

Moreover, it had gradually dawned upon workers and thinkers alike that the way of material argument—the argument of bomb and shell—was not the Ethiopian's way, and, in the world of progressive thought, the lamb was, after all, as the seer had foretold, leading the wolf and the lion instincts of the nations into right channels. It was a moral force with a moral persuasiveness which, like the wind, blowing whence men know not, yet was molding the spiritual atmosphere of the world. For what was to have become a great race war had become a mighty truce. The black races had at length learned to run along their own natural lines of development, and the white needed the black and the black needed the white. The work of Cain had given place to the grace of conciliation, and the West had called to the South and the South had responded in the thundering words of the great thinker, who said: "but if we fail in this?—If blinded by the gain of the moment we see nothing in our dark man but a vast engine of labor; if to us he is not a man, but only a tool; if dispossessed entirely of the land for which he now shows that rare aptitude for peasant proprietorship for the lack of which among their masses many great nations are decaying; if we force him permanently in his millions into the locations and compounds and slums of our cities, obtaining his labor cheaper, but to lose what the wealth of five rands could not return to us; if uninstructed in the highest forms of labor, without the rights of citizenship, his own social organization broken up without our having aided him to participate in our own; if unbound to us by gratitude and sympathy and alien to us in blood and color, we reduce this vast mass to the condition of a great, seething, ignorant proletariat—then I would rather draw a veil over the future of this land."

To sentiments such as these, ringing with deep sincerity and earnestness, workers and leaders on the Ethiopian platform could not but respond with equal sincerity and earnestness; and, in the mutual respect and confidence which resulted, the black man could call to the white man and say:

"Lofty I stand from each sister land, patient und wearily wise,
With the weight of a world of sadness in my quiet passionless eyes,
Dreaming alone of a people, dreaming alone of a day
When men shall not rape my riches and curse me and go away;
Making a bawd of my bounty, fouling the hand that gave—
Till I rise in my wrath and I sweep on their path and I stamp them into a grave.
Dreaming of men who will bless me, of women esteeming me good,
Of children born in my borders, of radiant motherhood,
Of cities leaping to stature, of fame like a flag unfurled
As I pour the tide of my riches in the eager lap of the world."*

* This is a quote from "The Law of the Yukon," a long poem by Robert William Service, a writer known as the "Canadian Kipling." Service's most famous poems are about the Yukon, a mostly wild territory in Canada. Casely Hayford is putting the words "spoken" by the land (as reported by the poet) into the mouths of the black man, who desires to partner only with those who are worthy.

Yes, it was a holy truce, and it was the spirit of humility which sealed it. It was one of those startling truths of life which men scarce realize when they hear it uttered. The late Henry Drummond emphasized this lesson in modern times in a way few had done before.* And yet he taught nothing new in this respect. To toil and moil for reputation, fortune, or position, and, when gained, to wonder at one's folly at having wasted so much energy and so much precious time is as old as the days of King Solomon who, in the plenitude of his power and might and dominion, wrote all down as vanity. And the converse way of life is as old as Socrates and the Pyramids; and Ethiopia can afford to take her part ungrudgingly in the arduous task of advancing humanity. The wonder is that, twenty centuries after Christ, the leading nations have not yet learned this great, yet simple, truth. And so it happens that they still toil and moil to make proselytes of other nations only to fill them with the unrest from which they suffer and to weary them with the burden which they bear. After years of patient waiting and discipline, Japan has at length shaken herself free from ancient conservatism, and China is following suit. As for India, she is even now in the grip of a great delirium. The lion and the bear are being threatened in their lair, and men can hardly believe their senses. And yet this is not the better part of Japan which wise men would wish to see perpetuated. Perhaps no one person, living or dead, did more to reveal the East unto the West than the late Lafcadio Hearn; and nowhere did the master-hand wield the magic wand more powerfully than in the living pages of that remarkable work, *Kokoro*, which "treats of the inner rather than of the outer life of Japan."† And herein lay the power of

* Henry Drummond (1851–1897) was a Scottish evangelist and lecturer. He was well known among religious and scientific communities for his published works, which included *Tropical Africa* (1888).

† Lafcadio Hearn, or Koizumi Yakumo (1850–1904), is credited with introducing Japanese culture, especially its literature, to the West. He was a journalist, translator, and writer. The quote is from Hearn's 1896 volume *Kokoro: Hints and Echoes of Japanese Inner Life*, in which the author states that his text treats "of the inner rather than of the outer life of Japan,—for which reason they have been grouped under the title *Kokoro* (heart)."

our author. He treated of the inner things of life. He belonged to that band of men who force their fellow men to think. They are not always popular; but whether or not, they are the saviors of the race.

Lest the temper of the people of the Gold Coast may be misunderstood, let it be premised that it is a remarkable thing that the date of Japan's political awakening has been noted to synchronize with the political awakening of the Gold Coast. Had the fates been propitious, the development of the latter might have been equally remarkable in its way. It is a curious fact, but one worth recording, that those who had the guidance, or, to use a more correct phrase, the protection of the budding aspirations of Fante nationality, noted early the symptoms of latent national possibilities, and, acting on the principle of *divide et impero*,* scattered the fragments to the winds. But the voice of the Creator has gone forth, and, even as the sea gives up its dead, so will the four winds blow back the hopes that were well nigh lost, and fan them into action. For, remember, that the Gold Coast people were contemporaries and brethren in institutions, language, customs, and practices, in the far interior, of the Ashantis whose polity, prowess and moral backbone have aroused the admiration of the world. For quite a century they were a martial power to reckon with, though without arms of precision; and when measures of repression have been removed, it is quite conceivable that their inherent virility will be turned into healthy channels of statecraft and race development.

It is, perhaps, not generally known that the Denkiras in the Gold Coast, occupying the country this side of the Offin River, whose capital town Gwikwa is close to Cape Coast, were once the masters of the Ashantis. The names of Amponsaim and Intsim Gakiri of the royal line of Denkira are well known in the history of Ashanti. There was a time when they inspired terror in the breasts of the Ashantis, and it was the haughty demand of Intsim Gakiri that the Ashanti tribute for a given year should be accompanied by a tooth of the king and his "best" wife that roused the Ashantis to the deadly

* More commonly, *divide et impera*: Latin for divide and rule.

struggle with the Denkiras which ended in the submission of the latter and their subsequent immigration to the Gold Coast, punctuated by a series of other political events.

And if you turn to the Fante portion of the Gold Coast, you find this, that they were one mighty host who broke away—*ifa wa atsiw*, hence their name Fante—from their brethren, the Ashantis in the hinterland and made their way to the coast. Now, when *Boribori Fante* came from Takieman, the *Abura Tuafus* led the van; but they were then not known as Aburas, no more were the *Anumabus or Akumfis* known by their present designations. They were all, as it has been explained, one mighty host under several great leaders who sat upon ancient stools in the interior. Their first care was to secure a suitable habitat for their gods, *Nanamu*. The god of rain, for example, was, and is, known as *Nana Yankum*. The first great center of the Fantes was *Mankessim*, meaning, the great city. As it was impossible for the hosts of *Boribori Fante* to abide together, soon a dispersion took place. It was reported among those who remained behind of those who went in the direction of Abura: "*Wo dzi hwon tsir abura mu nu hu*," that was to say, "they have taken some direction unknown," the name *Abura* attaching to the people from the verb *abura*. Likewise the Akumfis were so called from the density of the multitude, *Kumkumfi*, which separated from the main body and settled in the district now known as Akumfi.*

The polity of these people has been eloquently described by competent Fante writers, and in the pages of their works is seen a system of government at once harmonious, progressive, and sympathetic—a system capable of infinite development.

* Some accounts suggest that the separation of the Fante from other Akan groups happened around the thirteenth century. The Bɔrbɔr Mfantse group eventually migrated to Mankessim (in today's Central Region) under the leadership of three legendary warriors: Obunumankoma, Ɔdapagyan, and Ɔson. These migrants, too, were subsequently divided into separate groups. Today, Fantes are prominent in the Central Region along Ghana's southwest coast, though they can be found all over the country. The etymology Casely Hayford provides here is not the only known possibility.

Moreover, in the language of these people are certain characteristic root ideas. It is the language of poetry, and their unrecorded songs are full of the deep meanings constituting the soul of life. Take, for example, the word "*wireh*," meaning heart affection, in the phrase "*miwireh akitawu*," that is to say, "my heart is firmly knit to your heart." So familiar are they with the essence of the Godhead that you have ascriptions such as *Onumankuma*, meaning "*Onu a obotum de oka de Madaku ma*," that is to say, "he who can say, I alone am the giver," clearly corresponding to the eternal Giver of all good. Take another ascription, *Kwerampon*, meaning "*ekwerina ebira pun wa onye*," that is to say, "if you lean against him, none can sever you," clearly carrying the idea of "none can pluck you out of my hands." Now, whence these root ideas? They cannot be merely fortuitous, traceable, as they are, to the innermost consciousness of the people.

Thus it will be seen that the Gold Coast people are as good an Eastern type in some respects as those of whom we have written. Yet, today,

> *"Lofty she stands from each sister land patient and wearily wise."**

with a patience that marks for leadership in the spiritual realm.

Undoubtedly the highest form of character development attainable in any religion is that set forth in the graphic portraiture of Paul of Tarsus, where he makes true humility the door to the highest honor. And who can doubt it that, in this respect, Ethiopia, among the nations, typifies this aspect of the developed character today more than any other? In order to carry on her mission of peace what is wanted is the opportunity of intercommunication; and it is conceivable that some day it may be possible to reach Lake Chad from Northern Nigeria, and Kumasi to become a great center for converging lines of the Cape to Cairo railway. When that eventuality happens, and Ethiopia will have entered upon her universal spiritual mission, then, hoary with age, and freed from the trammels of so-called world progress, aims, and

* This is another excerpt from Service's poem "The Law of the Yukon."

ambitions, she shall pursue her onward path to God in the way of humble service to mankind; and, so, the saying of the seer shall become true that "a little child shall lead them."*

FINIS

* Isaiah 11:6, a prophecy about peace among different factions. The reader will remember that Kwamankra manages to use the same text as part of his wooing of Mansa.

Suggested Further Reading

Bernal, Martin. *Black Athena: The Afroasiatic Roots of Classical Civilization*. New Brunswick: Rutgers University Press, 2020.

Blavatsky, H. P. *The Secret Doctrine*. Edited by Michael Gomes. New York: TarcherPerigree Publishers, 2009.

Blyden, Edward Wilmot. *African Life and Customs: Reprinted from "The Sierra Leone Weekly News."* London: C. M. Phillips, 1908.

Cromwell, Adelaide M. *An African Victorian Feminist: The Life and Times of Adelaide Smith Casely Hayford, 1848–1960*. London: Frank Cass, 1986.

Danquah, Joseph Boakye. *The Akan Doctrine of God: A Fragment of Gold Coast Ethics and Religion*. Oxfordshire: Routledge, 2014.

———. "The Historical Significance of the Bond of 1844." *Transactions of the Historical Society of Ghana* 3, no. 1 (1957): 3–29.

Diop, Cheikh Anta. *The African Origin of Civilization: Myth or Reality*. New York: Lawrence Hill Books, 1997.

Falola, Toyin. *Nationalism and African Intellectuals*. Rochester: University of Rochester Press, 2004.

Frimpong, Kofi. "The Joint Provincial Council of Paramount Chiefs and the Politics of Independence, 1946–58." *Transactions of the Historical Society of Ghana* 14, no. 1 (1973): 79–91.

Hayford, J. E. Casely. *Gold Coast Native Institutions: With Thoughts upon a Healthy Imperial Policy for the Gold Coast and Ashanti*. London: Frank Cass, 1970.

———. *William Waddy Harris: The West African Reformer: The Man and His Message*. C. M. London: Phillips, 1915.

July, Robert. *The Origins of Modern African Thought*. Trenton: Africa World Press, 2004.

Kimble, David. A *Political History of Ghana: The Rise of Gold Coast Nationalism*. Oxford: Clarendon Press, 1963.

Masilela, Ntongela. *An Outline of the New African Movement in South Africa*. Trenton: Africa World Press, 2013.

Newell, Stephanie. *Literary Culture in Colonial Ghana: 'How to Play the Game of Life.'* Bloomington: Indiana University Press, 2002.

Nochlin, Linda. *The Politics of Vision: Essays on Nineteenth-Century Art and Society.* Boulder: Westview Press, 1991.

Odamtten, Harry Nii Koney. *Edward W. Blyden's Intellectual Transformations: Afropublicanism, Pan-Africanism, Islam, and the Indigenous West African Church.* East Lansing: Michigan State University Press, 2019.

Said, Edward W. *Orientalism.* London: Penguin Books, 2019.

Sarbah, John Mensah. *Fanti National Constitution.* London: Frank Cass, 1906.

Sekyi, Kobina. *The Blinkards: A Comedy; and the Anglo-Fanti—a Short Story.* Oxford: Heinemann, 1997.

Táíwò, Olúfẹ́mi. *How Colonialism Preempted Modernity in Africa.* Bloomington: Indiana University Press, 2010.

J. E. Casely Hayford: A Timeline

1866	Born September 29, in Anomabo
1891–1893	Served as editor at the *Gold Coast Chronicle* and headmaster at Wesleyan Boys High School at Accra
1893–1896	Studied law at Peterhouse, Cambridge, and at Inner Temple, London
1896	Called to the bar and returns to the Gold Coast
1902	Cofounded the *Gold Coast Leader*
1902	Cofounded the Fante National Education Fund
1903	Published *Gold Coast Native Institutions*
1911	Published *Ethiopia Unbound*
1913	Published *The Truth about the West African Land Question*
1916	Joined the Gold Coast Legislative Council
1919	Cofounded the Gold Coast National Education Scheme (for secular high schools) and published a pamphlet titled "United West Africa"
1927	Elected Municipal Member for Sekondi on the Legislative Council, founded Achimota School (with Casely Hayford as a member of the Achimota Council), and gave a speech to the Legislative Council on the death of Dr. J. E. K. Aggrey
1930	Died August 11, in Accra

Editors' Glossary: Additional Fante Terms

Akam yey: Good wishes, that the person who sneezed be sound of mind.

Akioo: Good morning.

Boribori Fante: The group of Fantes who migrated to Mankessim in Ghana's Central Region.

Ifa wa atsiw: (Disputed) etymology according to which the Fanti/Mfantse/Fante originated from the half (fa) that tore off (tsew) from the larger Akan group.

Kwerampon: The mighty, eminent one.

Kwiaduampon: The mighty one. Rendered by Casely Hayford as "the impregnable rock."

Miwireh akitawu: My heart is tied to yours.

Nyiakropon: An Akan name for God, the Supreme Being who is also the creator of the world. In the original text of *Ethiopia Unbound*, there are a few typographical errors/different spellings of this word.

Onumankuma: An appellation, used in this example to refer to God's generosity.